Freeing Fatima

MICHELE E. GWYNN

An M.E. Gwynn Publication

Cover by Emeegee Graphics

Editing: M.E. Gwynn

Contents

Chapter 1

The sun peaked over the horizon as Skyscraper slammed on the brakes. The van came to a screeching halt kicking up gravel on the edge of the road. His team leader, Captain Nathan James Oliver, code name, Outlaw, slapped the dashboard.

"What the hell?" He looked at the man behind the wheel.

"Sorry, Outlaw," he said. "Coyote. At least, I hope that's what it was." Marcus DuBose, aka, Skyscraper, rubbed his eyes. "They're still moving," he said, looking at the GPS clipped to the vent on the dash of the stolen van. It had been five hours since the chaotic firefight with the terrorists in Old Town Bucharest. They'd terminated the hit squad sent to kill them, thanks to the timely arrival of Cobra and his team, aided by their own man, Doc. When Doc went down from a bullet to the chest, the terrorists they'd been tracking ran taking with them the chemical engineering prodigy and hostage, Fatima Ali. There was no time to stop and think, no time to help Doc. Cobra and the SEALs stayed behind with their medic. Doc was their teammate, their friend, their family, and yet, they still had a job to do, and a high-priority kidnapping victim to rescue.

"As long as they don't ditch that damned car, we'll be able to find them." Outlaw looked over his shoulder into the back of the van. His men, Hank 'Hollywood' Jimenez, Allen Williamson, whom they called Ghost, and the two new temporary additions to his Special Operations Group, Lt. Shane McCall, aka Badger and his Chief Warrant Officer Nick Perrillo, code name Jersey, all sat slumped against the side walls, exhausted. "Everyone okay back there?"

"We were, until Skyscraper's shitty driving disrupted our nap," grumbled Hollywood.

"Shut up, Hank. I ain't having killing a coyote on my conscience." Skyscraper maneuvered the van back onto the road.

"You cut the throats of terrorists, but you balk at running over a damned wild dog."

Skyscraper threw a look at Hollywood in the rearview mirror. "Coyote ain't done a thing but be a coyote. He hasn't killed innocent people. I'm not about hurting animals, just evil-ass terrorists."

"Okay, okay, that's enough," said Outlaw. "We need to catch up. If I'm not mistaken, they're heading for Chisinau and the international airport there. We crossed over into Moldova about twenty minutes back." Outlaw held up the map on his screen showing it to the men in the back.

"But where are they going? Where do they think they can fly with a hostage?" Ghost asked.

"Most likely they have a plane waiting. If the Saudi Crown Prince's brother is indeed the one orchestrating this then that means Prince Nayef would have the means to provide safe transport out," said Badger.

"A private jet," Skyscraper mumbled. "Oil billionaires never travel any other way, right?"

"And that's why we need to catch up because once they get onto the tarmac, we won't be able to stop them," Outlaw pointed out.

"Roger that Captain." Skyscraper pushed the gas pedal to the floor. The van sped up tearing down the deserted back road in a race against time. "She saw me, you know."

"What? Who?" Outlaw looked at Marcus.

"The girl, or young woman, I should say. She looked right at me before they shoved her into the car. Screamed for me to help her."

"And we will, Marcus. We are." Outlaw patted his shoulder.

"Damn right we are. She's strong, though. I could see it in her eyes. Pretty eyes," he said, his voice dropping to a whisper before he clammed up once again to focus on driving.

Outlaw's eyebrow came up. Skyscraper didn't often say much. The tallest, and deadliest of his team members was usually quiet, reserved. When he did speak, it carried weight because his observations had, on more than one occasion, led to their team's success and saved lives. He'd never once heard the younger man make this kind of comment before regarding the subject of a mission. It struck him as odd, but then, the entire mission had been one surprise after the next. His thoughts drifted to Doc, last seen lying on the ground, blood staining his vest. He sent a silent prayer up for his friend, and then sent another back home to his wife, Emma. The baby was due at any moment, and he knew he'd never forgive himself for not being there when it arrived. He still didn't know if it was a boy or a girl. They'd decided to wait and see, to be surprised. There was too much on his mind, too much to worry about, but right now, he had to focus on rescuing this woman. She was the priority. Everything else would fall in line.

Chapter 2

The landscape changed. She could see it through the tear in the hood tied over her head. Fatima Ali tried to quiet her mind as she sat as still as possible in the corner of the sedan. Three men were in the car with her. One was almost dead having caught a bullet in the terrifying firefight hours earlier. She'd first heard the commotion from inside the filthy hotel room where she'd been held for days. Shots rang out alerting her captors who scrambled for their guns. The leader of the group, a pock-faced man called Omar, had pushed her down on her knees next to him as he peered out a crack in the window blinds.

Outside, it sounded like a warzone. The cacophony of bullets had her covering her ears. Her heartrate skyrocketed in fear, but she reached deeper for comfort focusing inwardly on the words of her mother. *"Listen to your breath, Fatima. Concentrate on it. In. Out. In. Out. No one can take away your calm but you. Keep your breath and keep your head.*" These were the wise words of Sulima Ali spoken ten months ago. That was the last time she saw her mother after they were taken. It was during a visit to her father's family in Syria. There, with the entire country under siege, men claiming to be the opposition against the Al Assad regime had come calling. In short order, they revealed themselves to be imposters. ISIS recruiters. They killed her uncle and then her father. They took her and her mother intending to ransom them, but then, the one called Omar recognized the work badge in her mother's purse and everything changed.

Calls were made and then Omar and his men took her and her mother to another location. They stayed there one week, kept in a small room with little food or water. Only enough to keep them from starving. At the end of the week, three new men showed up. They came into the room with Omar who then informed her mother she would be going with them.

"No!" Fatima remembered her loud cry, remembered the terror that seized her heart.

Omar slapped her hard. "Shut up, girl!" He looked at Sulima Ali. "You will be working for us now. You will do as you are told, or we will kill your daughter. You understand?"

Sulima only nodded, gently pushing Fatima behind her. "You will not hurt her or by God, I will kill you myself," she said.

Omar laughed. "You are a disgrace before Allah, Christian. But before you burn in hell, you will help our glorious revolution." This was not the first time he'd derided their belief in Christianity. Syrian-born Christians were rare. Many chose to leave the country rather than stay and be persecuted. That was the choice her father and mother had made before her birth opting to live, instead, in Dubai.

Sulima had turned then to her daughter, cupping her face. "Do not cry. Do not show them they have won. They cannot break you. God will keep you safe, I know it, and I will find you, Fatima. I love you, my daughter. Always." She'd pulled her into a tight hug, fighting back the tears.

Omar pulled them apart and the three men dragged her mother from the room.

The knot that formed in Fatima's gut had stayed there since, but instead of letting it weigh her down, she drew strength from it. In her mind, the knot was her mother's love, a never-ending ache and a constant reminder not to give up. From that day on, Omar had been cruel, but he'd kept his two men from molesting her, obviously on the orders from someone higher up. She endured his perpetual insults and occasional beatings when she couldn't hold her tongue any longer. She did not regret striking out at his fragile ego. She'd discovered early on he was overly-sensitive about his pock-marked face. When his cruelty became too much to bear, she let her own verbal barbs fly.

"It is no wonder you're so angry all the time. What woman would ever put up with you with that face. It would likely cause her nightmares." Retaliation had been immediate. The strike sent her flying back, but as she nursed her red, pained face, she smiled. It infuriated him.

Months had passed with the cycle of isolation, insults, and beatings repeating. Until last night, she'd lost all hope. And then she'd seen him. Fatima did not know who the man was, but his eyes caught hers and somehow, she knew her nightmare would soon be over. She'd heard their voices, their words. Americans. They were American soldiers. There was no doubt now that they would rescue her. No doubt he would free her, whoever he was. In her heart and mind, she was sure her mother had discovered a way to fulfil her promise. She'd sent an army to save her.

Now all she had to do was wait for an opportunity to run.

"You are very quiet for a change, Fatima." Omar's voice interrupted her thoughts.

"I have nothing to say," she said, squinting to better see through the small tear in her hood. The landscape began to give way to civilization. They were approaching a city.

Omar sniffed. "But you will soon have much to do. Our benefactor has requested your presence."

She tensed. "My presence?" Alarm bells went off inside her head.

"Yes. And for your sake, you had best be as useful as your mother was."

Fatima's heart stopped. *Was?*

Omar's hand shot out, gripping her chin beneath the hood. He yanked her face around to his and leaned in, noticing the tear. "It's your turn. Where we are going, there is no turning back. You will be his, no longer under my control. Will you miss me, Fatima?"

His voice dropped low as his fingers dug into her jaw. She knew better than to answer. He was baiting her, as usual. But as usual, she couldn't help herself.

"Not for one moment."

She braced herself for the hit. It didn't come.

"This will be our last time alone, Fatima, and since you are already damned, Allah will look the other way and forgive my transgression." He grabbed her, quickly sliding her down on the backseat beneath him.

Fatima screamed, swinging wildly, her hand connecting to his face. Immediately, she dug her fingernails into his cheek, raking the skin and drawing blood. In the front, the driver, Mufid, kept his eyes on the road, ignoring the commotion. The one slumped in the passenger seat was already dead.

"Get off me, you dog!" She kicked, her knee barely missing his groin.

This time, he did slap her. The blow stung and knocked the hood off her head.

Able to see now, she fought like a wildcat as Omar reached down to pull up her skirt.

"No!"

"Stop fighting, bitch, or I'll kill you!"

"Do it! Kill me! Then this benefactor you're so afraid of will demand answers and you will be the one responsible!" She kicked again.

Omar grabbed a handful of her long, black hair and yanked until her neck bent back exposing her throat.

Fatima sucked in air, trying to breathe through the pain.

"Such a beautiful neck," he said, and then licked it, still pulling up her skirt.

The car swerved and a hail of bullets hit the vehicle. Two tires blew out and Mufid lost control of the wheel. The sedan went off the road into a field, tearing through shrubs before landing in a ditch.

Fatima was thrown to the floor on top of Omar. He was knocked out cold, a bloody gash in his forehead visible from the impact.

The side door opened and the barrel of a rifle peeked in.

"Don't shoot!" Fatima covered her head, squeezing her eyes shut as fear seized her.

"Miss Ali?"

She heard the voice, deep and soothing. She glanced up. The gun barrel was gone. In its place, warm amber eyes sought hers. A hand reached in, large and strong.

"Take my hand," he said.

She reached up, taking the offered hand, her own trembling. It was as warm as his eyes. He pulled her out, careful to guide her away from the body beneath her. In the front seat, Mufid lay slumped over the wheel now shoved tight against his chest. He wasn't moving. With a shudder, Fatima crawled over Omar into the arms of a very tall man. Standing on shaky legs, she looked up...and up some more.

"Thank you," she whispered. The dry air coupled with the adrenaline rushing through her body made her cough. He patted her back. Regaining her composure, she looked around at the group of men surrounding the car. "You are

American soldiers," she said, her words a statement rather than a question.

"Yes ma'am," said the tall one. "Sergeant Marcus Dubose." He pointed at himself, then looked to the man with piercing blue eyes. "That's Captain Oliver, our leader, and these men are Hollywood, Ghost, Badger, and Jersey."

Fatima nodded. "Very colorful names. Very American, I suppose."

Marcus shrugged. "They're nicknames. I have one too."

Her focus returned to him. "And what is your nickname?"

Marcus grinned. "Skyscraper."

She nodded. "I see. Which do you prefer?"

"Whichever you're comfortable with is fine by me, Miss Ali."

"Then, thank you, Marcus."

Skyscraper cleared his throat. "You're welcome, Miss Ali."

She reached up, touching his chest, gratitude in her eyes. "Fatima. You must call me Fatima."

"We need to get out of here before someone drives by," Outlaw said.

Skyscraper nodded, gently taking her hand. "Miss Al—Fatima, we need to go."

"Where are we going?"

Skyscraper looked at his leader. Outlaw glanced at Ghost.

"Call Rio. We need a safe route out of Moldova. Tell him we have a Plus One." Outlaw pulled Skyscraper and Ghost aside, away from Fatima. "We still have a leak situation inside COM-SAD. Until we get a head's up that they've secured the mole and plugged the leak, we need to stay under the radar. That means Miss Ali is our responsibility. We need to hide her somewhere where Prince Nayef won't think to look for her, and where she'll be safe from any IS operatives."

Skyscraper looked at Fatima. Hollywood and Jersey stood beside her. Badger checked the bodies in the car. He poked the two in the front seats.

"Dead," he said.

"I can take her home." Skyscraper spoke, still looking at the young woman.

"Home?" Ghost's pale brows rose.

"New Orleans," he said. "We just need a VISA and passport. Think Rio can arrange that? No one will think to look for her there and we can wait out this storm."

Ghost looked at Outlaw who shrugged. "See what Rio can do. With our cover blown, being back inside the U.S. is the smartest move."

"New Orleans it is, then." Ghost pulled out his burner phone and walked to the van. Behind him, the men escorted Fatima Ali to the back of their stolen vehicle. Badger quickly took pics of the dead to send back to his people at Black Site Alpha for identification. As soon as the van door slid shut, the lieutenant poured accelerant onto the wrecked sedan and lit a match. He ran, jumping into the passenger seat as Ghost drove them to safety. The sedan went up in flames. No one saw the man limping away into the ditch before the fire hit the gas tank. The explosion sent debris flying in every direction.

Chapter 3

Skyscraper studied Fatima's face from behind dark sunglasses. Despite the past forty-eight hours spent traveling non-stop, including a side trip to a small German town of Oranienburg near Berlin, she appeared alert and unruffled. When they arrived in Germany—a whirlwind trip of stolen cars and rail travel from Moldova—they were tasked with locating a man called Olaf. A Swede in lederhosen is what Rio called him, and apparently a trustworthy counterfeiter of documents of every variety.

The Swede lived in a typical Germanic house, one that reminded Skyscraper of Bavarian-styled gingerbread houses from the Hansel and Gretel fairytale. The house was a block away from Sachsenhausen, a defunct Nazi concentration camp still open to tourists. They spent two hours with Olaf who forged a German passport and VISA for Fatima under the name Tina Mueller. It even had a couple of stamps showing travel two years prior to both

France and the UK. With her paperwork taken care of, they moved on, taking the rail to Brussels where Marcus purchased Fatima some American-style clothing and a small suitcase. A woman traveling to America without luggage would bring unnecessary attention to them. The men all had duffel bags stuffed with a few items as carry-ons, but she needed her own. She would be traveling on the same flight out to Atlanta's Hartsfield, but she would be sitting alone, separate from them to avoid suspicion.

She did well, and it was to her credit she spoke decent English. In the time it took to make it safely back into the states, she'd remained quiet. Her composure was solid, but there was sadness in her brown eyes. That bothered him, although he couldn't explain why it mattered. The sadness lifted once they arrived in New Orleans replaced with avid curiosity. After securing two taxis, the group made their way to Tremé, the neighborhood where Marcus had been born and raised.

His mother and sister weren't expecting them as he'd had no time to get in touch. There was also the fact he didn't want to give anyone a heads-up of his whereabouts, not with an unplugged leak within COM-SAD. First stop needed to be for lodging. He couldn't just show up at his mama's doorstep with a bunch of hardcore soldiers and a Syrian engineering prodigy expecting to stay in the small three-bedroom shotgun house he'd grown up in. It would be bad manners. So would showing up without some kind of a gift. Food was always acceptable and even expected. That meant a stop-over at the Parkway Bakery on Hagan for a Butter Rum Cake. It was Magnolia Du-Bose's favorite, and the only thing she loved more than her children. As a single mother, she'd raised Marcus and his younger sister, Jasmin, mostly on her own. His father, Richard J. DuBose, known as Richie Keys in the Tremé, left them to pursue his music career. He died from a fatal heart attack only two years later never quite realizing his dream nor fully knowing his children.

This affected him more than he would ever admit. He'd watched his mama struggle to put food on the table. When he graduated high school, joining the military was a no-brainer. He still sent half his paycheck home to help her out. Magnolia was getting too old to continue working full time. Arthritis was slowly but surely crippling her joints, and the money paid the bills and helped put his sister through college.

As the taxi pulled up to the bakery, he noticed the longing on Fatima's face. She came from a different world than the one in which she now found herself. It seemed unfair not to let her experience a little bit of the goodness that was New Orleans.

He turned to Outlaw. "We're not far from the hotel, and my mama's house is within walking distance from there. I think it might be safe to let the taxi go. Besides, the fellas could use some good soul food. Might put some color in Ghost's cheeks," he said, glancing at the pale soldier. Ghost flipped him the bird, but smiled, not the least bit offended. "We can catch another cab afterwards."

Hollywood leaned up in the backseat. "Please, dad!"

His tomfoolery made Outlaw's eyes roll.

Badger chuckled. Jersey unrolled the window and inhaled the amazing aromas emitting from the restaurant. His stomach grumbled loudly.

Ghost waited patiently, but his hand was already on his duffel bag, ready to jump out.

Outlaw's stomach let out its own groan. He sighed. "Yeah, okay. Let's eat. Get whatever it is you feel we need to bring to your family, and then we'll check into the hotel."

"Don't get yourself too excited about that place, Captain," said Skyscraper. "The Tremé Hotel isn't the Ritz by any stretch." He opened the car door while Ghost paid the cab drivers.

"As long as there are four walls, a bathroom, and a bed, I'm not complaining," said Outlaw.

"Good, because that's about all it's got." Skyscraper helped Fatima out, offering her a look of apology. "But at least you'll eat well tonight."

She stretched her arms above her head, inhaling the foreign scents coming from inside the Parkway Bakery. "I have no complaint, Marcus." She dropped her hands to her sides before reaching back inside for her suitcase.

"I got it," he said, reaching around her and pulling the small blue case out. His shoulder brushed hers as they bumped together. "Sorry," he said.

"Excuse me," she muttered, casting him a sideways glance.

"My fault," said Skyscraper. He hefted his duffel bag over his shoulder and carried her suitcase in his other hand. With only an elbow free, he offered it to her, a gentlemanly gesture drilled into him from childhood Sundays escorting Grandmama Rosemary, his maternal grandmother, to church.

Fatima smiled, sliding her small hand into the crook of his arm. Together, they entered the busy restaurant.

Behind them, Outlaw and Hollywood exchanged a look. Ghost suppressed a grin and Badger and Jersey shook their heads.

Over the next hour, the group enjoyed a wonderful meal and camaraderie with a backdrop of jazz provided by a local band. Once the waitress delivered the Butter Rum Cake, boxed up and ready to go, they caught a mini-van cab, and squeezing in, headed to the Tremé Hotel. The plan was simple. Check in, rest an hour, and then head over to the lavender house on N. Roman Street, the one with a fifty-five-year-old magnolia tree in the front yard planted by his mama when she and his father first married. As exhausted as Skyscraper felt, he was excited to see his mama and sister again.

※※※※ ※※※※

On N. Roman Street, a black Toyota Highlander pulled to a stop. It sat parked across from a lavender shotgun house with a tall, shady magnolia tree in the front yard. Engine off, the driver, hidden behind tinted windows and a sun visor, watched as an old black woman came out the front door. She reached into the mailbox mounted next to the door and pulled out a handful of envelopes. She flipped through them unaware of the eyes upon her. After a moment, she turned, heading back inside. As soon as she was no longer visible, the man known on Interpol watch lists as Omar Baz signaled to a second man in the backseat. Both the one in the backseat and the one currently sleeping in the passenger seat wore the traditional long beards of

Muslims. A stark contrast from the clean-shaven face of the man calling the shots. It was necessary to the mission to blend in. His orders were clear, procure the girl or face execution. Omar did not doubt it. The Saudi prince was not prone to half-measures. If he failed, his death would be slow and painful, and deserved. Their cause was all that mattered. For that, they needed an expert bomb maker. With the mother out of play, it was time for the girl to prove her usefulness to the Islamic State. And if he succeeded, the prince might offer him a reward. Omar's lips thinned into a sinister smirk. He knew exactly what he would ask for...to take the prince's bomb maker as his concubine.

"Salib! Wake up!" Omar reached out, smacking Muhammed bin Salib's cheek. The younger man snorted awake.

"What is it," he replied, speaking his native language.

"Stay alert!" Omar looked at the man in the backseat, Muhammed Daher Tahan. "Do you have everything ready?"

The husky, bearded man nodded. He held up a length of rope and a syringe, then pointed at the grenade launcher laid out on the seat behind him. "We are ready."

Omar grunted, reaching out to smack Salib again. "At least one of you is worthwhile. If I catch you sleeping on the job again, I'll see to it you never awaken."

Salib swallowed, nodding. "My apologies. It won't happen again, Omar."

"Good. Take the wheel and park there," he pointed, "and wait. Stay out of sight." Then, he and the man in the backseat got out of the Highlander. Looking both ways, they moved quickly crossing the street. They dropped low by a hedge and made their way down the side of the house, disappearing from view.

Chapter 4

Fatima sat on the edge of the bed in her hotel room. It was as unimpressive as Marcus said it would be, and yet, she felt safe. It was the first time in a year she'd felt this way, and she had him to thank for it. The threat she'd lived under, the violence of assault and death, died in that car in Moldova. She looked down. Still wrapped in a white towel after a hot shower, she could see the most recent bruises fading from bright purple to a mottled green. Those would be gone soon, but the scars remained. Omar had made a game of putting his cigarettes out on her back and over her breasts when she displeased him, which was often.

Some were faded to white on her tan skin, but others were still fresh, pink, and puckered. In two months, she would be twenty-four, and already, she'd lived through a lifetime of torture that no one should ever experience. The trauma of her abduction was compounded now by the fact that her mother was dead. When Omar first spoke of Sulima Ali in the past tense, she hadn't had time to fully process what he'd said. She'd been fighting off his attempted rape. Then the car crashed, and she was rescued. It was too much happening all at once, but now, sitting here alone in the quiet, run-down hotel room in New Orleans, the pain seeped into her soul and her control snapped. Fatima wept. She curled into a ball on the side of the bed, sobs racking her as her heart broke. What would she do now? Where would she go? With both her father, and now mother gone, there was no one. She was an orphan and had no one. The reality of her plight, the overwhelming pain of it all, flowed out in a river of tears she was sure would drown her. And she would welcome her fate, for it was better than living without the love and protection of her family.

***

Skyscraper put on fresh clothes. Jeans, a black t-shirt, and a pair of black athletic shoes. The shower refreshed him, washing away the sweat and dust of travel. Dressed once again with his duffel bag repacked, he stretched out on the low bed. As usual, his feet hung off the edge. At 6'7", it was impossible to find a hotel bed big enough for his size.

He'd grown used to it. It only mattered when he slept on his back. Rolling to his side, he could draw up his legs until his feet were on the mattress. It didn't matter right now. Fatigue settled into his battle-weary body. He stared at the ceiling fan through heavy-lidded eyes, then, rubbing them with the back of his hand, looked around the room.

The dingy walls were partially hidden by the shadows cast from the closed curtains. He could still make out the stains in the far corner of the ceiling near the door. A water leak. Someone had slapped a coat of paint over it but failed to hide the damage completely. As he looked at it, a sound reached his ears. In the room next to his, a low keening penetrated the thin walls. Fatima was crying.

Blinking the grit from his eyes, he stood, automatically reaching for his sidearm and then remembered he didn't have one. They'd ditched all weapons before getting on the plane out of Brussels. They had to use their alternate passports, IDs unknown to anyone outside of their immediate commander, General Davidson, which meant they couldn't be caught carrying military weapons. These were the passports they carried for extreme emergencies. This was the second time Skyscraper had to adopt the identity of civilian Terrence Murphy instead of Sergeant Marcus DuBose. His hand dropped back down to his side and he sighed. He glanced at the nightstand and reached for the knife placed there.

Adapting to their lack of weapons, he'd taken advantage of the dinner cutlery at the Parkway Bakery restaurant, pocketing a steak knife. He'd left an extra $50 in the tip to make up for his petty theft. Ten dollars for each missing knife. All six men now had a shiny, sharp blade. He was sure the busboy cleaning up after their meal might have wondered why out of seven diners, only one knife remained on the table. Or maybe he hadn't noticed at all. Not everyone was trained to pay such close attention and most civilians were oblivious to their surroundings.

The stainless-steel steak knife had a solid black wooden handle. He picked it up off the nightstand and slid it into a leather sheath he kept handy. The sheath attached to his waistband through a belt loop. He hooked it to the left side. Then he slid his keycard into his jeans pocket. Exiting the room, he looked both ways and eyed the parking lot below. They were on the second floor near the stairs. The way was clear. He moved left approaching Fatima's door. Skyscraper raised his hand to knock and paused. Suddenly, he was unsure what to say. Her cry might be a private moment he shouldn't intrude upon, or she might need help. For what, he didn't know. What if she'd hurt herself? What if she was in pain? He didn't like the idea of Fatima in any kind of distress, not after everything she'd gone through. Usually, by now, someone from the military or the State Department would've taken over her care, would've been interviewing her, finding out about her kidnapping, attending to her, but this wasn't a normal situation.

They couldn't just hand her over because of the mole. Doing so could put her life in danger and theirs as well. It was on him to make sure she was okay. A decision reached, he knocked.

"Fatima, it's Marcus," he said. Earlier, he'd told her not to open the door to anyone except him or Outlaw. His captain occupied the room on the other side of hers, a room shared with Ghost. Hollywood, Badger, and Jersey had rooms at the foot of the stairs on the first floor with Badger and Jersey sharing. They'd spread out like that forming a strategic block on the end of the building. It was a classic damsel in the high tower formation.

The door opened, chain still on. Large brown eyes peeked out through the crack.

"Yes?" she said.

Skyscraper placed a hand on the door jamb. "You okay?" He noted the fresh tear tracks on her cheeks.

She nodded, taking a deep breath. "As well as can be expected, I suppose," she said, reaching up to slide the safety chain out of the lock. Opening the door wide, she backed up.

Skyscraper moved inside, closing the door behind him. He noticed her state of undress and forced his eyes to remain focused on her face. "I think you're exceeding expectation. You've been through a lot. We would've taken you to help, to some medical professionals, but things aren't normal right now. I'm sorry about that, but if you'd like to talk, I'm a good listener."

She swallowed, her full lips stretching into a humorless smile. "I don't think I can find the words, Marcus." She moved to the bed, sitting down on the edge and clutching the towel tight around her body.

Skyscraper followed, sitting next to her. "I hear you. Kidnappings are nightmares that never go away no matter how hard you try or how strong you are. None of it was your fault. Not a single minute of it. You know, those men can't ever hurt you again. We made sure of that."

She looked at him. "That's not it. That's not what is," she clutched the towel over her heart, tears blurring her vision, "hurting so much."

Confusion filled Skyscraper's amber eyes. "Then what?"

Fatima's throat tightened painfully. "My mother," she whispered.

"What about her?"

Tears flowed as she broke down. "She's dead. She's dead, Marcus. She promised she'd find a way to save me, and I know somehow she did, but now she's dead and I'll never see her again!" Sobs racked her body once again.

Skyscraper watched the strong young woman crumple inward upon herself. He reached out, wrapping his arms around her, trying to understand.

"Who told you she's dead?"

Through her pain, Fatima mumbled, "Omar, right before the car crashed into the ditch. Right before you saved me."

Skyscraper silently cursed the dead terrorist. He patted Fatima's back before lifting her chin to face him. "Fatima, your mom isn't dead." He wiped away the fresh tears from her eyes. "You're right. She's the reason we found you. We found Sulima Ali by accident tracking ISIS's new bomb maker. We rescued her and she claimed asylum with the United States. It was because of the information she gave about your abductors that we were able to find you. Your mom is safe and sound in Washington, D.C. As soon as we're able, we'll reunite you."

The pain and disbelief in Fatima's eyes turned to a tentative hope as he watched. Her entire being lit up. "Truly? You're not lying?"

Skyscraper held up two fingers. "Scout's honor. I'd never lie to you. She's alive."

Fatima threw her arms around his neck, hugging him tight. "Oh, my gosh! Marcus, thank you! Thank you, thank you, thank you!" She began to cry again, but this time, from happiness.

He chuckled. "Happy to help, but you might be soaking my shirt back there," he said. He didn't really mind. She smelled heavenly, like lilacs and sunshine. And there was something about holding her close that just felt right.

"Oh, I'm so sorry." Sniffing, she pulled back, looking up at the kind soldier with the warm, amber eyes and bronze skin.

"It's okay." He smiled, flashing a dimple.

Fatima reached up, touching the indention. "A well of laughter," she said.

"What's that?" Skyscraper's eyebrow arched.

"You call them dimples. I call them wells of laughter." She sniffed back the last of her tears and smiled. "The deeper the well, the more the bearer laughs. Yours is deep, but you only have one." She let her fingertip trail away, her hand dropping to his chest.

Skyscraper cleared his throat. "Yeah, well, my mom has the same dimple. I guess we share the laughter." He sat up, putting some distance between them.

"That's very sweet. I can't wait to meet her."

"She'll like you," he said.

"How do you know."

He looked at her large, almond-shaped brown eyes. The long lashes cast shadows on her cheeks in the waning light of late afternoon making them appear longer than they already were. "Because I like you."

Fatima blushed, her black hair sliding forward like a silken curtain to cover her face as she looked down. Warmth filled her soul and she peeked at him shyly. "I like you too, Marcus."

The moment stretched. His heart racing, Skyscraper raised a hand, reaching—

Fatima inhaled, standing up. "Thank you for checking on me. What time will we be leaving to go to your mother's home?"

Skyscraper's hand dropped to his side as he got up quietly berating himself. "An hour. That should give us all enough time to rest up, which reminds me, I need to call her. If I don't give her a heads-up, she'll have my head," he chuckled. "I'll knock in an hour. Remember," he said, opening the door and stepping out of the room, "don't open this for anyone except me or the captain."

Fatima moved closer, her hand on the doorknob. She smiled. "I know. Only you, Marcus."

His eyes dropped to her lips as she spoke his name. "Um, yeah," he said, shaking his head. "Or the captain. But none of the other knuckleheads!" He shook a finger at her, joking. "They're shifty."

"What? Marcus, they're your teammates!" She raised a mocking eyebrow.

"And that's how I know they're shifty. But only around beautiful women. Other than that, they're okay. One hour, Miss Ali. See you then." He closed the door before she could reply.

Fatima stood staring at the safety chain swinging from the wall, her mouth hanging open. He'd called her beautiful. The compliment may only have been given out of politeness, she was sure, but still... She'd discovered her mother was alive, and the kind soldier with the warm, amber eyes called her beautiful. Joy and gratitude filled her soul.

His voice carried through the wall. "And put on that chain lock!"

Grinning, she slid the chain home, her heart fluttering.

Chapter 5

Lt. Shane McCall, aka Badger, responded to the beep on his burner phone. He opened the text message and, memorizing the six-digit code, swiped over to the internet where he logged into the dark communications site through an obscure dating ap for seniors. Entering the code, he navigated to the account for #thirstyB. There, he opened the private messenger. A report began to download. Sitting up, he reached across the open space between his bed and Jersey's.

"Nick, wake the fuck up!"

Nick Perrillo snorted. He wiped his face and threw Badger side-eye showing his irritation at having his sleep disturbed. "What?"

Badger turned the phone screen in his direction. "Black Site Alpha got readings on the dead."

"So?" Nick rolled over. "They're dead. Why do I give a fuck?"

"Because one of 'em ain't dead, apparently."

Nick rolled back, sitting up. "What are you talking about?" He reached for the phone.

Badger handed it over. "Omar Baz. He was the one in the back seat. BSA database identified him. They also flagged him arriving by private jet at Louis Armstrong International two hours before we arrived!"

"Didn't you check him? I know I heard you say they were all dead. And you blew up the car! How's that possible?"

"I don't know, man. I checked the two in the front seat, but I couldn't reach into the back. He was on the floor. I poked him with my gun barrel. He didn't move. Either way, he should've died in the fire. We did hightail it out of there. He could've gotten out if he was still alive. I fucked up. This is bad. We need to tell Outlaw. Now."

"Shit!" Nick jumped up, grabbing his carry kit and tossing another to Shane. After they'd checked in earlier, he caught a cab to a local hardware store picking up the necessary items. Rake picks and tension wrenches for picking locks, compasses, a couple of miniature flashlights, fishing wire, and from the pharmacy next door, Zebra pens, a couple of lighters, a carton of cigarettes, and some mouth nightguards. He'd handed them out to the men, each putting together their own carry kits. The hotel had free cheap razors on the bathroom vanity. He'd removed the razors and rolled them up in a handkerchief. A couple of rolls of ace bandages and duct tape were used to secure phone books and hotel room bibles to their chests—makeshift Kevlar. They'd had to request an extra one of each. The lie rolled easily enough off Jersey's tongue when he'd told the desk clerk there were none in the room and that he'd feel much better having the good word of God nearby. It was a partial truth, one that may not entirely repel a bullet, but would slow it down and help protect vulnerable internal organs in a firefight.

"Shit, indeed. He knew right where to come which means he was listening back there in Moldova. That leak at COM-SAD needs to get plugged ASAP. These assholes have more than Outlaw's team's identities, they have the families too."

"The Captain is gonna be pissed. That was a rookie mistake. You're better than that, Shane. We don't call you Badger for nothin'."

"I know, Nick. All I can do now is fix this shit. He should've died yesterday. I'm a day late in sending that fucker to his maker."

Badger secured the ace bandage with a couple of layers of duct tape and pulled a black t-shirt over his head covering the homemade protective vest. A second button-down shirt in blue was pulled over that, sleeves rolled up. "We need fire power. Think Hollywood procured us some handguns yet?"

"Let's go find out. He should be with us when we tell Outlaw about Omar. He might be less inclined to kill us both with one of his own there."

"As if Hollywood would stop him. Goddammit, I deserve this." Badger shook his head, mentally kicking himself. Jersey was right. It was a rookie mistake; one he'd not normally make. Always make sure the bad guys are dead. No matter how still they lie, put a bullet in their head anyway. Just in case. He hadn't. Instead, he took the lazy way out. No other word for it. He'd grown too used to being on base interrogating suspects and had been too long out of the field.

"Stop whining and let's go fix this." Jersey slung his carry kit over his shoulder. To any outsider it simply looked like a man-purse. A leather carry-all with a long, cross-body strap. His Italian machismo had balked at the idea of carrying one when he first began training for special operations, but his C.O. told him to grow a pair. *That purse will save your life, Perrillo, and the lives of others in a tight situation. Spec Ops sometimes have to go black, get off the grid to survive and everything in that fucking 'purse' will help you live to see another day so get over your preconceived bullshit notions about gender and accessories now."* That had been the end of that conversation, and many off-the-grid situations later, his C.O.'s words proved true.

Jersey tossed a second leather cross-body bag at Badger. "Here. Take your purse, bitch."

Badger pocketed his cell phone and caught the bag. He sent Perrillo the finger and grabbed the room key card. "I think I'm about to find out why they call the captain Outlaw. Fuck."

They stepped into the corridor and walked next door to Hollywood's room, knocking. They were greeted with the business end of a Sig Sauer 9-millimeter.

Badger glared at Hollywood. "I see your hunting expedition was successful. Mind getting that out of my face?"

Hollywood lowered the weapon, chuckling. "It was. Got one for each of us," he said, turning back to the room. He pointed to the bed. Laid out across the cover were five more Sigs, AR-15s, Bowie knives, ammo for the guns, two-way radios, and camo bandanas. "It was all I could carry." He shrugged.

"Knocked off a local gun shop?" Jersey asked, reaching for one of the handguns. He grabbed a pack of clips, shoving one into the gun.

"Yeah. Should be on the news later, I'm sure. Only the clerk and one customer inside at the time. Left them both tied up comfortably."

"What kind of distraction did you leave behind?" Badger asked, selecting his handgun and picking up one of the semi-automatics.

"I spray-painted 39 on the wall."

Jersey raised an eyebrow. "Meaning?"

Hollywood sighed. "Local gang. The 39ers, man. Research. It's a thing."

"Good job, Hollywood," said Badger. "Listen, there's been a development. We need to inform the captain right away. You need to be there. All of us need to be there, actually."

"Sounds serious," Hollywood said, cocking his head.

"It is. Fuckin-A serious," said Jersey. "And urgent."

"Then let's go. We can come back for the goodies," he said, taking the AR-15 from Badger. "Leave that here until you have something to hide it under." Hollywood gave a pointed look to the Lieutenant's t-shirt and roll-sleeved button-down.

"Yeah. That can wait, but the information can't. Let's go. We'll grab Ghost and Skyscraper on the way."

Outlaw read the report on Badger's phone. His brow creased and anger lit his blue eyes. In the time it took the men to assemble in his room, yet another alert had come across the backchannel. Two more terrorists from the CIA watchlist had entered the U.S. enroute to Denver, Colorado. He'd immediately called Rio.

"Send MP's to my house and get Emma out now!"

"Already done, Nate." Rio heard the panic in his friend's voice. "She and the baby are at base HQ and under guard."

"What?" Outlaw stopped pacing. "The baby?"

Rio chuckled. "Aw, damn. I guess Doc didn't tell you before he took that bullet. He's okay, by the way. He didn't stay in the hospital, though. Checked out AMA to get back to Colver and that redheaded gal that stole his heart. But yeah, you're a papa. You have a son. Don't know his name, but ten fingers and ten toes. They're both doing well."

"I have a son," said Outlaw, dropping down into a chair.

"Already informed Doc too. He and his family have been taken to Fort Carson. Damned terrorist threat interrupted his engagement party."

"Doc popped the question? Holy shit!" Outlaw looked at his men.

Ghost patted Outlaw on the back. "Knew he would. He was a smitten kitten from jump. And congrats on your baby boy."

Hollywood gave him the thumbs up while Skyscraper grinned, quiet as usual.

Badger and Jersey exchanged a look, grateful that some good news softened the blow and might save them a beat-down.

Outlaw caught them and glared, his expression clearly saying they weren't off the hook. "Thanks for looking out for us, man. I owe you."

"A beer," said Rio. "You know I've got your back. CIA already have agents waiting at the gate to arrest these two bastards. Federal Air Marshalls were on it. They detained them an hour ago. No casualties. Interpol also caught two more boarding in Paris for the U.S. One heading to California, Hollywood's family, and the other to Washington, Ghost's hometown of Seattle."

"That's good news. When I see you next, all drinks are on me. Now what about the ones here? Omar Baz and the two Muhammeds?"

"Baz is the leader. Muhammed bin Salib and Muhammed Daher Tahan are low-level IS recruits. State Department wants Baz. The other two are expendable."

"Roger that. Any news on the mole?"

Rio grunted. "We're narrowing down the field. Having to work with one of your old faves on this."

"Who?"

"Adam Jones."

Outlaw felt his blood pressure rise at the mention of the name. The last time he had to deal with Jones, Emma wasn't yet his wife. She'd been kidnapped once already and was under threat by Al Waleed and Black Jihad. Adam Jones tried to get him, and his team, taken off the assignment, but thankfully, General Davidson wasn't having any of that. He knew better and so did Outlaw. "That self-righteous prick? For God's sake, why him?"

Rio snorted. "Fuck if I know. Secretary of State is too busy. Sends her aide in to coordinate. He's a first-class idiot, that's for sure. Doesn't seem to understand how a sting op works. Keeps making stupid suggestions. Wrong directions and wasting my time. I've taken to just doing what I know needs doing and ignoring him for the most part."

"Don't be fooled, Rio. He's a wily bastard. Full of ambition. There's not much he wouldn't do to get ahead and that includes fucking you over. Be careful."

"I know his type. And I always cover my tracks. Got Natalie Greenblatt helping. Her experience in Intelligence is helpful, plus, she's a far better contact at the SD. The icing on the cake is it pisses Jones off when I go over his head. Don't you go worrying about little ole me, Nate. It's not my first rodeo. I'll find the mole."

"Good. That bastard put my family in danger," said Outlaw, looking at Badger, "and I don't take kindly to anyone who does so."

Badger shifted, guilt eating at him.

Armed with new information and orders, Outlaw wrapped up his call. "Thank Cobra and the boys for me. I really appreciate them taking care of Doc."

"Will do. When this shit is all said and done, all of you need to come visit. I'll barbecue. Bring your son so I can start telling him all the juicy tidbits about his daddy. Oh, and Rio is a fine name choice, by the way."

Outlaw chuckled. "Nice try, buddy, but there's no way I'm naming my son Rio."

"Hater," he laughed. "Rio out."

Outlaw hung up and faced the men. "You heard most of that. What you didn't hear is that the threat to your own families has already been neutralized."

Ghost and Hollywood looked visibly relieved.

Outlaw continued. "And we have new orders." He turned the screen of Badger's phone out facing them. The grainy CCTV security image taken at Louie Armstrong International showed three men coming through customs.

"This one is Omar Baz, the dead man walking who got away." His sharp blue eyes pinned Badger's. "State Department wants him. The other two are non-essential."

The men nodded, understanding that the other two would soon be wearing toe tags.

"Captain, I'm sorry."

Nate eyed Shane. It was obvious apologies from the Lieutenant were not easily given. The anger simmering within caused by sheer panic for Emma's and his child's safety cooled a degree. "Prove it, Lieutenant, by correcting the mistake."

Badger straightened, recognizing his chance to make things right. "Will do."

Skyscraper's thoughts strayed to Fatima who was alone next door in her room. "So, what's the plan?"

Outlaw looked at his man. "Baz will be heading to your address, no doubt. I don't know your family, Marcus. You do. Tell me, will informing them of the threat panic your mother and sister or should we not tell them and just find a way to get them out quickly?"

Skyscraper's eyebrow rose. "Nothing ruffles Mama's feathers. But I don't like her being left in the dark. She was fine when I spoke with her half an hour back, but a lot can happen in that time. I'd rather she know. She preached preparedness to me growing up. She won't panic, she'll plan."

"Then call her now. Tell her what's up and that we're on the way. Just act normal. Don't do anything that might alert these trash bastards that we're on to them. They may already be watching the house."

Dread slithered down Skyscraper's spine. He pulled out his phone, dialing. "I'll filet the fucker who hurts my mama and sister."

"And I'll help," said Badger.

"Ghost, Hollywood, we need a car." The two men nodded, heading out. Within fifteen minutes, Ghost returned.

"Found a nice Suburban looking for a new owner. Ready?"

Outlaw nodded. The men left the room stopping to get Fatima and making a quick run into Hollywood's room. Armed with weapons and Buttered Rum Cake, they piled into the stolen vehicle and headed to the lavender shotgun house on N. Roman Street.

Chapter 6

F ear snaked up Fatima's spine as Marcus explained about Omar. He'd survived and he was coming for her. She closed her eyes and tried to breathe, tried to find her calm, but the trick her mother taught her wasn't working. Her whole body shook, reacting with panic. A hand closed around hers, strong fingers intertwining with her own. The calm she'd been seeking seeped into her limbs. Fatima glanced sideways. Marcus looked straight ahead, but his hand held hers tight.

With one touch he was telling her he would not let anything happen to her. She knew without a doubt he would stand tall against any threat to protect her. She studied his profile from his prominent cheekbones to his strong jawline and full lips. He was a handsome man to behold. He kept his hair cut short like military men do, but she could see the slight wave in the black strands. Marcus had an interesting mix of features that reminded her of the

Native Americans she'd read about and Louisiana Creoles. She wanted to ask him all about his family, to be able to enjoy a conversation where they might get to know each other. She wondered if they would ever get past this threat to her life so she might once again live without fear.

He seemed to read her mind as he caught her watching him. He squeezed her fingers.

"Don't worry, Fatima. Everything is going to be alright. I'll keep you safe."

Warmth spread throughout her body from his touch and tingles danced down her spine. It was both disturbing and exciting. Her experience with the opposite sex was limited to a few stolen kisses with a boy from university. She'd been only seventeen upon admittance, one of the youngest ever to be enrolled in the advanced biochemistry and engineering program, and the only female at the time. Fatima knew it was all due to her mother's connections, but she'd been fully aware of the privilege that allowed her, even in the more progressive Dubai, to move forward in her studies. It was there she'd met Amin, an Egyptian exchange student. He was cute, kind, and funny. One afternoon in the library, deep in the stacks searching for Introduction to Chemical Engineering Thermodynamics, the book that would make or break their careers the next semester, he'd pulled her close and kissed her. It was her first kiss and as she recalled, very sweet but a bit disappointing.

Fatima had never been wildly romantic, but every girl hopes for the type of kiss that knocks her socks off. Amin's kisses were pleasant, but they didn't fire up her core like a nuclear reactor. In fact, they hadn't caused nearly as much excitement as Marcus's simple touch was doing now.

She didn't know if it was the impending danger, his proximity, or what, but in that moment, all she could focus on was his lips. She cleared her throat and pulled her hand away.

"I'm okay," she said, sitting up straighter.

Next to her, Hollywood chuckled. He looked over her head at Skyscraper whose face reflected confusion at her withdrawal. "I never thought I'd see the day," he said, shaking his head.

Outlaw glanced back over his shoulder, looking at the three in the backseat. "What are you talking about?"

Hollywood grinned and began singing, "another one bites the dust."

"Shut up or I'll kill you in your sleep, Hank." Skyscraper's quietly spoken words penetrated Hollywood's off-key singing. He stopped immediately, throwing a look at his captain.

Outlaw's brows rose in amusement. He turned back facing forward once again saying, "Emma will be happy to hear it."

Skyscraper rolled his eyes and shook his head before looking out the side window. Beside him, Fatima wondered at the men's exchange even as a blush burned her cheeks.

The scene on N. Roman Street was a sight to behold. It looked like the entire block had descended upon the lavender shotgun house. People stood on the lawn beneath the magnolia tree which was adorned with bright party lights. Two men stood by a large grill on the gravel driveway. Smoke billowed from the grill's chimney as the men sipped cold beverages. Another group of men lined the sidewalk casually talking with their neighbors. It looked for all the world like a block party, but a second look revealed more. Each of the men wore yellow vests with the words 'NEIGHBORHOOD WATCH' stitched in blue thread across the back, and each yellow vested man, and even some of the wives, wore holsters packed with handguns, some carried rifles.

In the middle of it all stood Marcus's mother. The petite woman wore a bright pink dress and block-heeled pink Mary Jane shoes. A colorful hat bedecked with a purple feather capped off the outfit, but it was the antique Winchester rifle she held that stood out.

"You did say she would plan," said Outlaw, his expression incredulous.

Skyscraper chuckled. "That's mama. Always prepared. I see she rallied the troops."

Ghost parked the Suburban in front of the gravel driveway. Skyscraper got out and turned to lend a helping hand to Fatima. Hollywood, Outlaw, Badger, Jersey, and Ghost exited the vehicle coming around to join them.

"Marcus!" His mother raised her hands, shotgun in her right fist, and jumped up and down. "Praise Jesus, my baby is home!" She came at him, a blur of pink and purple stopping only when she wrapped her arms around Skyscraper's waist.

"Hi, mama," he said, laughing, returning her hug and leaning down to kiss her cheek.

She reached up, touching his face. "Let me look at you." Smiling, she sniffed back tears. "Handsome as ever, but Marcus, you're too skinny! That's okay, we got some barbecue grilling, and I made my potato salad and cornbread. Jasmin's making more sweet tea. Oh, I'm so happy to see my baby boy!" She looked around at the men and then her eyes lit upon Fatima. "And who is this young lady, son?"

Marcus stepped back from his mother and reached for Fatima's hand, pulling her closer. "Mama, this is Fatima Ali. Fatima, this is my mama, Magnolia Dubose."

Marcus's mother gave the young woman the once-over, her eyes missing nothing. "Um hmm. Yes, she's lovely, Marcus. About time you bring someone home," she said, reaching out to engulf Fatima in a hug.

"Mama, she's not—"

"Welcome to our home, Fatima. And don't you worry. I know Marcus can't tell me everything," she said, shooing her son away as she turned herself and Fatima towards the house, "because he's one of them super soldiers that does all them secret missions, but you are safe here. See? I got the whole neighborhood to come over and make sure of it. Let's get you something to eat. Then we'll have a little girl-talk." Magnolia Dubose stopped, looking back over her shoulder. She handed the Winchester to her son and nodded at the men. "Ya'll are welcome too. Come on in and grab a plate. Then head inside to the kitchen. Marcus will show you the way. We'll talk there. I'm expecting better answers, you hear?" She marched away taking Fatima with her.

"She's a pip, your ma," said Jersey, laughing.

"This is the craziest thing I've ever seen." Badger took in the scene, shaking his head.

"But effective," said Ghost. "Smart thinking on your mom's part. Omar and his sidekicks wouldn't dare roll up on this crowd."

"Even without the neighbors they would've been out-matched," said Marcus, hefting the Winchester. "My sister has a 9mm pistol and a Browning. Trained her myself."

Hollywood looked at the Winchester. The name Peter was etched into the old wood with the numbers 5:8 next to it. "And she named her rifle. I like your mom already."

Skyscraper grinned. "Something like that. It's a Bible verse, you damned heathen. *Be sober-minded; be watchful.* It says the devil is always on the prowl like a hungry lion seeking prey to devour. Great-grand-pappy Isaiah's Win-chester gets blessed by the reverend once a year. Mama keeps it by her bed. She's fired it twice to my knowledge at intruders. Once when we were just kids. Some burglar tried to come in the back door one night. He got the scare of his lifetime. Sent him running across the backyard and over the fence, probably shitting himself."

"And the other time?" Hollywood asked.

A wicked gleam entered Marcus's amber eyes. "My sister dated a real loser about two years back. She finally saw the light after he cheated on her. She broke it off, but he kept trying to come around. Jasmin came home one night to find him waiting for her in the driveway. She didn't have a handgun yet. The fool was drunk and belligerent. Mama heard them arguing and came out, Peter in hand, and fired a warning shot in the air. The drunken idiot pissed himself. I mean, literally pissed himself. He was so embarrassed he never showed his face again. That's when I took a short leave of absence. Came home and took Jas to the firing range, taught her how to shoot, taught her about weapons. She's sharp, my little sis. I think if she ever chose to, she'd make one helluva sniper, but that ain't happening. She's going to college. Gonna become a lawyer specializing in civil rights."

Hollywood smiled. "You're very proud of her."

"Damn right I am. And don't you even think about hitting on her!" Skyscraper poked a finger in his face and then pointed at Badger and Jersey. They backed up.

"Why do you always lecture me and not Ghost?" Hollywood asked.

"Because Ghost knows how to be respectful to women. It's your ass I gotta watch." He threw a look at Badger and Jersey. "And you two, I don't know well enough yet, but be warned. Jasmin is off limits!"

Ghost laughed, patting Hollywood on the back. "You'd act the same way if it was your sister, Hank."

"I don't have a sister," Hollywood conceded. "But yeah. Probably,"

"We have orders from Mrs. DuBose," said Outlaw, refocusing the men on the mission. "Men, grab a plate and let's head inside. We have plans to make and a terrorist to catch.

Chapter 7

The dining room was crowded. For this reason, Magnolia DuBose ordered her son and his men into the small kitchen conducting the move like a seasoned maestro.

"Hank, you grab those two chairs against the wall and Captain, you get two folding chairs from the closet behind you. That'll be enough for all of us. Emmet," she said, turning to the old gentleman wearing a yellow vest who was currently refilling his plate in the formal dining room, "you watch this door and make sure no one comes in. If anyone tries, send out the signal."

The old man nodded, reaching for a slice of cornbread. "You got it, Miss Magnolia. No one's gettin' past me." He straightened, adjusting the strap of his Browning rifle over his shoulder.

Outlaw gave the man the once-over as he hefted two folding chairs on one arm. Mr. Emmet looked to be around seventy years of age, sporting thick glasses and arthritic fingers. His face must have reflected his skepticism because Skyscraper smirked, leaning in to whisper, "Don't let Mr. Emmet's age fool you, Captain. He's retired army. A decorated sniper for Korea and Vietnam. Even with those Coke bottle lenses, he can shoot a hair off a fly's ass a mile away."

"You don't say?" said, Outlaw, impressed.

"Mr. Emmet taught me how to shoot when I was just a young buck. He's one of our church deacons now, but growing up, he was kind of a father figure. They don't make 'em like him anymore."

"I heard that, Marcus," said Charles Emmet, chomping on his cornbread. He wiped the crumbs from his lips, smiling. "And it's true. They don't make 'em like me anymore. But I'd like to think I did a pretty good job with you."

"Hearing still works too, I see," said Outlaw, chuckling. "I'll just take these into the kitchen then."

Skyscraper placed an arm around Emmet's shoulders. "You did, Mr. Emmet, and there isn't a day that goes by that I'm not grateful for you."

Emmet grinned, shooing him towards the kitchen. "Go on with you! I got things under control here. You go do what needs doing because whatever it is that got Magnolia gathering the troops is surely dire. Handle your business, son, and remember what I taught you. Stay focused and keep God in your heart."

Skyscraper tapped the bible strapped to his chest beneath his clothing. "Always, sir."

He was the last to arrive in the small kitchenette; a yellow and cream wallpapered room. His team sat uncomfortably close. Ghost, Hollywood, and Jersey side by side on the banquet bench bumping elbows. Outlaw and Badger sat in the folding chairs on the opposite side next to Fatima and his sister Jasmin. His mother held court at the head of the table leaving the last chair on the other end for him. Catching sight of her big brother, Jasmin jumped up throwing her arms around his neck, hugging him tight. He hadn't seen her for over a year and she looked beautiful as always. His little sister stood 6' 1". Height ran in the family, but not from his petite mother. It was Richard DuBose who passed on that gene.

"Good to see you, big brother," said Jasmin. She whispered into his ear, "and you've got some dirt to spill later on the exotic hottie."

Skyscraper gave his sister a light pinch. "Nothing to tell, Jas, now hush."

His sister was unfazed, slapping his hand and pointing a finger at him. She wagged it in a taunting manner while suppressing the grin threatening to spread across her lovely face.

Fatima watched the exchange between brother and sister noting their similarities. Marcus's sister also had light amber eyes with long lashes. Her skin was a few shades lighter, but she shared the high cheekbones of her brother in addition to the height. Jasmin was beautiful with long, curly hair worn loose and flipped over to one side. She didn't have the single dimple of her brother and mother, but her smile lit up the room. Wearing jeans, a green Tulane University t-shirt, and adorable green and gold sling-backs, she looked like a model. Fatima glanced down at the blue button-down shirt with rolled sleeves paired with an ankle-length floral skirt in shades of blue on a white background and her white canvas sneakers. She tugged the shirt hem tied at her waist and shifted uncomfortably in the straight-back chair. She was unaccustomed to American fashion. Most of what she'd seen since arriving showed the women of this country unabashedly showing off their bodies. Many opted for body-hugging blue jeans, tight tops, and short dresses, clothing that would be deemed unacceptable in the UAE.

Across the table, she noted Hollywood and Ghost watching Marcus's sister. Both men tried to go about it surreptitiously, appreciation reflected in their eyes.

"Now that everyone's here, I believe the captain should tell us what it is we need to do." Magnolia DuBose had removed her hat before sitting down at the head of the table. "Captain?" she said, looking at Outlaw.

The captain nodded, taking over. "First, thank you, Mrs. DuBose, for having us here. I know this is the worst of circumstances. I'm sorry for it and I appreciate you letting us into your home." The older woman nodded, smiling. Outlaw continued. "Our original intent was to stay at the hotel until our command brought us back in, but now that we know not one but three terrorists on the government's watchlist have entered New Orleans," he said, leaving out the fact that several more also entered through other ports of entry and were now in the custody of the State Department, "we need to change that plan. It's clear they know where we are and they know who you are," he said, looking at Jasmin and Skyscraper's mother. "We didn't anticipate this, but now that we have the intelligence, we can't leave you unprotected. That said, I'm not familiar with your city. However, Marcus is so I'm going to defer to him." Outlaw looked right at Skyscraper. "No one knows better how to defend this house than you. No one knows this neighborhood better than you do. We'll need to set up choke points, so, Sergeant, where should we begin?"

Skyscraper sat forward. While he wasn't surprised his commander would seek his advice based on his own first-hand knowledge of the area, he was thrown that Outlaw would have him put forth the strategy. He glanced at Fatima. She looked at him with so much trust. He knew he couldn't let her down. He couldn't let any of them down. Not his sister. Not his mother. Not his team, and right now, all were in danger. He hated that what he did brought danger down upon their heads. And he never wanted his mama to see the soldier side of him. It was forged in brutality, and Magnolia DuBose had not raised him to be violent. Quite the opposite, actually.

When neighborhood bullies threatened a young Marcus, she advised him to turn the other cheek, to try and understand what hell they might live in at home to make them so angry and mean. It was good advice from a good-hearted woman, but not practical. When he'd taken his first beating in middle school, receiving a bloody nose, he didn't run home, but next door to Mr. Emmet. It was there he learned how to defend himself. Mr. Emmet didn't advocate for violence either, but he didn't shy away from it.

"Sometimes, Marcus, despite your best intentions, you won't be able to walk away. Bless yo mama. She's a wonderful woman, but she can't always be there to protect you.

Now," he'd said, taking the young man outside in the back-yard, "it's time you learn a thing a two about how to deliver a proper beat-down. Just don't tell your mama," he'd whispered. "She'll kill us both!"

Here he was today in yet another situation where running away had not helped. But now, he was a man, and mama needed him. So did Jasmin. And, he glanced at Fatima, so did the beautiful Miss Ali. He thought about the neighborhood layout, where both ends of N. Roman Street met cross-traffic. Leaning forward, he spoke, outlining a plan. They would fortify at four points laying traps. After that, it would be a waiting game. Omar Baz and his henchmen would make a move. They had to. It was the reason they'd followed him and the team to the U.S. And when they did, their attack would be met with deadly force.

Chapter 8

After the neighborhood watch left, Fatima was shown to a room. It was just to the right off the back-entry door. The room itself was a small space with two narrow but high windows on the wall opposite the door. There were posters on the walls of athletes from the American football team, the New Orleans Saints. She was not familiar with the Americanized version of football, sparing them only a glance, but a corner of one wall caught her attention. There, displayed amid purple and gold masks were three framed pictures with writing on them. Stepping closer, she studied them with interest.

"Those belonged to our dad," said Jasmin, who'd come up behind her.

Jasmin had shown her to her brother's old bedroom. After the meeting in the kitchen, he'd asked his sister to take Fatima there so she might rest up while he and the team set up their surveillance for the long night ahead.

She suspected it was more of an effort to get the civilians out of the way, but the fatigue in her body told her it was welcome, nonetheless.

Fatima stared at the images of musicians. "Who are they?" Two of the pictures were autographed.

Jasmin leaned in. "This one is Ellis Marsalis Jr. He's a famous jazz pianist, but also an educator at the New Orleans Center for Creative Arts. Our dad once played with him at a local club here in the Tremé. I guess that's where he got the autograph. This one down here is Kermit Ruffins. He plays trumpet. Still does a lot of festivals here. And that one," she said, pointing at the gold-framed picture at the top, "is our dad, Richard DuBose. People called him Richie Keys."

Fatima took in the details of the tall, black man sitting at a piano surrounded by fellow musicians playing trumpet, trombone, and saxophone. A drummer in the background had his hands raised ready to bring the drumsticks down, but it was Marcus's father that commanded attention within this moment in time caught on film. He was sitting on a piano bench, one long leg stuck out to the side while the other tapped the pedals beneath the keyboard. He faced out to the crowd, a big smile on his face as his fingers played across the keys. He wore a simple suit in an indistinguishable dark shade, the faded colors from the old image long ago losing their vibrance. His white shirt was unbuttoned at the neck, but even with the age of the film she saw the strong resemblance between Marcus and his father.

"And where is he now?" Fatima asked.

"Dead," Jasmin replied. Her voice held no pain. "I was too young to remember. He walked out and left us when Marcus and I were just kids. His music was more important to him than his family. He died a couple years later from a heart attack. I think I was five. Marcus was ten. He remembers our dad. All I have are some pictures. This is one of the few of him performing we own. There's also an album somewhere around here. Richie Keys cut a few tracks with some local jazz musicians, and they put it out. Didn't sell a lot, but it was his only claim to fame before biting the dust."

The unemotional explanation was unsettling. Fatima still felt the keen loss of her father. Tariq Ali was a kind man who worked hard all his life to provide for his family. His jovial and loving nature made him a wonderful dad and as his only child, she'd enjoyed his undivided attention. When Omar and his men put an end to his life and that of her uncle, it felt like her heart had been ripped from her chest, and yet, she hadn't had time to mourn. She'd been abducted along with her mother and had been fighting for her own life since.

A light knock interrupted her reverie.

Fatima turned to find Marcus standing in the doorway. He gave a pointed look to Jasmin who threw up her hands, smiling.

"Alright, big bro. I'm going." Jasmin reached out touching Fatima's shoulder. "I'll be down the hall at the other end if you need anything."

"Thank you, Jasmin." Fatima watched the tall young woman walk past her brother gently knocking his arm with her shoulder saying, "behave yourself, Romeo."

When they were alone, Skyscraper stepped in, closing the door leaving only an inch of open space. He glanced around the room, an amused expression lighting his amber eyes.

"Weird to be back in my old room. Seems like a lifetime ago when I hung these old posters."

"You don't enjoy sports anymore?" she asked.

"I haven't had time, really." Skyscraper looked beyond Fatima to the pictures of musicians on the corner of the far wall. "Haven't had time for that either."

"What, your father's memory?" she asked. "I am sorry to hear of your loss, Marcus."

He smiled. "Thank you, but no, not that. My dad passed a long time ago. My memories of him are few and far between. What I meant was music."

"Oh, yes. I'm not familiar with jazz music. I guess you do not get many opportunities to listen to it when you're working."

A deep chuckle escaped his lips. "No, I don't. Nor do I get any chances to play it."

This surprised Fatima. "You play piano?"

He stood beside her looking at the image of his father. "Yeah. It's one of the few gifts I inherited from him," he said, "and one of the few memories. Pops used to sit me next to him at the piano at the club where he played. Always during the day when rehearsing. He taught me the keys. Later, long after he'd passed, mama sent me next door to Mrs. Emmet's house. She played for our church choir. Mama could see how down I was after Pops died. She knew it was the one thing he and I had together, so she asked Mrs. Emmet if she'd continue my musical education. That's how Mr. Emmet became a father-type figure for me. I spent more time at their house as a boy than I did here at home. She made the best macaroni and cheese casserole too."

Fatima heard the love in Marcus's voice as he shared this part of himself. It made her feel closer to the quiet, handsome soldier. "I would very much like to hear you play sometime."

Skyscraper cleared his throat. "That might prove painful to your delicate ears. I'm out of practice."

"I'm sure it would come back to you." Fatima reached out taking one of his large hands into her own. "They are very strong and capable hands," she said, her warm fingers wrapping around his palm. "And you are a strong and capable man. You saved my life, Marcus. I can never thank you enough." She gazed up at his face.

Skyscraper felt himself getting lost once again in the warmth of her eyes. "No thanks necessary. Just doing my job."

"But it wasn't. You said so yourself. My mother was your mission. You found her. You didn't have to come after me. Didn't have to chase Omar all over the Middle East and Eastern Europe for me. Marcus, when I first saw you in Bucharest, I was terrified. Bullets flying every which way, grenades exploding, and Omar dragging me out into the middle of it all." She paused. "I saw you and I just knew..."

Skyscraper stared into her upturned face. Her deep brown eyes were filled with emotion. "Knew what?"

"I knew you would save me. I never believed in fairytales as a child and the only heroes I knew were my father and mother. But there you were, so tall, strong, and fearless.

You saw me. And you came for me." Her words ended on a whisper.

Skyscraper felt his heart flip in his chest even as his gaze fell to her lips. They were naturally red and lush and all he could think about as she held his hand was how much he wanted to kiss her. The urge was overwhelming, but he fought it. She was in his care, still under threat. It would be wrong to take advantage when, to his estimation, she clearly hadn't had any experience with men. Not with her conservative upbringing. And after everything she'd been through at the hands of the terrorists, much of which he still did not know, he'd be a first-class horse's ass to give into his own selfish desires.

Fatima, however, had other ideas. As Marcus began pulling his hand away, she released it, reaching up with both arms and sliding them around his neck. With surprising strength, she pulled him close and pressed her lips to his. It felt like kissing a live wire, but in an exciting way, and then the sparks turned to delicious flames spreading throughout her entire body.

Good intentions went out the window the moment Fatima's lips found his. Their softness and the heat emanating from her curvy frame nearly brought him to his knees. His arms slipped around her waist pulling her tight against his body. He was unmanned by the honesty of her passion. He let her steer the kiss where she wished, but at the first tentative touch of her tongue, he took over. One hand slid up, his fingers delving into the silkiness of her long hair, cupping her head as he gently angled in, tasting the sweetness of her mouth.

Fatima melted into him. Nothing had ever felt so right. A strange yearning grew within, and she wanted more. She sighed, allowing him deeper access and he did not disappoint. Hands roamed, caressed, kneaded even as he moved them both slowly to the twin bed in the corner. There, he pivoted around sitting down on the edge. She felt his fingers reach down and slide up her lower legs to her knees beneath the long skirt. Those same fingers gently but firmly pulled her astride fitting her snugly on his lap against his hips. Her skirt was now scandalously high revealing strong, slim thighs. When his lips moved to her neck, she moaned.

The sound of her pleasure was an intoxicating aphrodisiac. His body responded, growing hard. He forgot about Omar, about the mission, about everything except the feel and the taste of this sweet woman. He gripped her hips, wanting so much more.

The insistent hardness now pressing against her core caused a deeper groan to escape her lips. Fatima felt both hesitant and excited. Before now, her experience had been a few sweet kisses and then the abuse by Omar and attempted rape. It was a broad spectrum of extremes, neither of which prepared her for this, an all-consuming desire to merge her body to another's. This must be what the priests had warned about at services. Getting carried away. Fingertips skimming her thighs clouded her thoughts and she thrust her hips seeking more.

Skyscraper was nearly gone, his passion rising to a fever pitch, but a voice in the back of his mind nagged at him. His own damned conscience was telling him to slow down, back off. The voice changed to that of Sulima Ali's saying she trusted him, and then it morphed into his own mother's familiar tone pointedly stating she'd raised him better than to take advantage of a young lady. He pulled back, taking a deep breath while lifting Fatima off his lap. He placed her on the bed beside him.

"Hey, what—"

A knock on the door cut off her words.

Clearing his throat, Outlaw spoke through the crack of the doorway. "Sergeant, move it out. We're setting up the backyard surveillance now." With that, the captain went out the back door.

Skyscraper knew he needed to go, but he hated leaving Fatima after their encounter. He wanted to tell her why he stopped. There was no time. Outlaw's words were an order and he'd never failed to respond to one before. He would not start now.

"I have to go." He stood, absently tugging his pants to relieve the tightness. When that didn't work, he untucked his shirt from his jeans pulling it down to hide the evidence of his desire.

Fatima straightened her clothes. While she understood he needed to obey his commander, she struggled with a feeling of rejection. She squared her shoulders and lifted her chin. "Go then. I'm fine."

Skyscraper paused. He'd been raised by and around women and he knew better than anyone that when a woman says she's fine, she's anything but. The defiant tilt of her beautiful face confirmed what he already knew. Fatima was hurt. He attempted to smooth things over. "I'm sorry, Fatima. I'd stay if I could. I'll be right out the backdoor tonight. Please stay inside. It's the only safe place right now." He turned to leave and stopped at the door. "We'll talk tomorrow."

"There's nothing to talk about, Marcus," she said, getting up and approaching the doorway.

"Yes, there is," he said, noting the heated flash in her dark brown eyes. "Like the fact that I hate that I have to leave, and the fact that you're mad that I'm leaving." He reached out, touching her face. "The only thing making me walk out this door, besides my captain's order, is the fact that a dangerous fucking terrorist is out there right now coming for you. I can't let that happen. I have to put Omar out of commission. Then, and only then can we revisit this," he said, leaning down and capturing her lips in a quick, hot kiss. "Believe me, beautiful, I'd rather be here."

Skyscraper walked out the back door, locking it as he went. His parting words drifted through the small panes of glass embedded into the top frame of the door. "Don't open this for anyone—"

"But you," she whispered.

Outside, Skyscraper smiled. He'd heard her although she hadn't meant him to. There was hope. But first, he had two terrorists to terminate and one to capture. And his pants were still uncomfortably tight. It was going to be a long night.

Chapter 9

Inside the lavender shotgun house, Fatima paced the short length of Marcus's room. His words did help her feel a bit better. Deep down, she knew he wasn't leaving because he wanted to, but it still stung. She was also suffering a bit of embarrassment over the fact that his captain obviously knew what they'd been up to when he knocked. Her body was still thrumming with desire, but the more she paced, the faster it cooled. And as her womanly bits stopped jumping up and down for attention, her brain began to work once again.

She hated feeling helpless. She's spent the last year under guard, tormented, abused, with no way to help herself. Now, she was free, mostly. Other than for her own safety, no one was telling her what to do. Even though Marcus and his team were outside doing all they could to protect her and his family, she didn't think it fair not to do her part. All she needed was a weapon or two. For that, she needed a few items. It was time to show the American soldiers why she was such a high-profile target. With her mind made up, Fatima left the small room and marched down the hallway in search of Jasmin. She felt confident that Marcus's sister would agree with her plan and help her gather the necessary items to build her own improvised weapons.

She was right.

"Girl, just tell me what we need." Jasmin was onboard. She showed Fatima her Sig 9-millimeter handgun.

"That will help, but it won't be enough. I need my own weapons. Also, I don't want to kill anyone, just incapacitate them." Fatima grabbed Jasmin's hand and led her out of the room heading towards the kitchen. "We'll need a disposable camera if you have one and lighters and duct tape." She rattled off a list.

Jasmin grinned. "Damn, this is some MacGuyver shit!"

Fatima paused. "Who?"

"Never mind," Jasmin waved off the question. "Just saying this is some genius-level badassery."

Grinning, Fatima nodded. "You must teach me the meaning of your words later. Shall we?"

Marcus's sister grabbed Fatima's right arm lifting it high in the air. She high-fived the younger woman. "Let's go Amazon warrior women on these bad guys."

"Indeed. We'll teach them not to underestimate the fairer sex," Fatima laughed.

"Damn right, sister." Jasmin bumped Fatima's hip with hers playfully.

After a scavenger hunt throughout the house, the two women closed themselves up in Marcus's room and began assembling not one, but two improvised tasers having discovered an old pack of disposable cameras in a drawer, and three improvised flash-bangs from old lighters. If Omar or his men managed to get past the American soldiers stationed outside, the women would be ready for them. Two hours had passed when Mrs. DuBose poked her head into the room to check on Fatima. The surprised look on her face when she beheld the weapons on the nightstand was replaced with curiosity. After Jasmin explained, Magnolia DuBose smiled, patting both girls on their cheeks.

"Never let it be said that women are incapable. We're survivors through and through." She turned to her daughter. "Jas, help me get the blue easy chairs in here. Then I'll get my Winchester and we gals are gonna hole up in this room and ride out this storm. It's going to be alright, girls. Jesus has our backs."

Unable to sit still, Fatima joined the women in dragging two over-stuffed recliners down the hall and into the small bedroom. Once situated, Magnolia, who'd changed into a silver track suit and running shoes, sat down promptly pulling the lever extending the leg rest.

"Whew! Mama's tired, girls." She rested the Winchester across her lap. "Ole Pete here is now on duty."

"Don't worry, mama," said Jasmin, "I'll take first watch. You grab a nap." She pulled a green throw blanket off the end of the twin bed and laid it across her mother's legs.

"I'll stay up with you, Jasmin," said Fatima. She pocketed one of the two improvised tasers and kept the flash-bangs at hand on the nightstand. She handed the second taser to Jas. "You can attach it to your belt loop." Fatima showed her the lanyard retractable clip she'd tied to the disposable's wristlet. "This way, your hands are free to shoot and the taser is handy when you need it. Just grab, pull, and aim for the body. But make sure you turn it on first here." She performed a mock demonstration.

"Got it. Thanks." Jasmin sat in the blue recliner closest to the door while Fatima sat cross-legged in the middle of the bed. Between them, a soft snore emanated from Mrs. DuBose's lips.

"I hate this, the waiting," Fatima said. "A whole year of it and my patience has not improved."

"What happened to you?"

Fatima shrugged. "Terrorists killed my father and my uncle while we were visiting my grandmother's home.

They took my mother and me, and when they discovered who my mother worked for, they forced her into making bombs for them. She only agreed to save me. I was their leverage, but also, their backup. You see, I was enrolled in university earning my biochemistry and engineering degree. Like my mother before me, I have a gift for the sciences." Jasmin's eyes went wide. She leaned forward waiting to hear more of Fatima's story. "Anyway, they kept us separated. My time with them was...almost too much to bear." Fatima swallowed, remembering the abuse, the torture, and the despair.

Jasmin went to her, wrapping her arms around the younger woman. "Sssh, you don't have to tell me anymore."

"No, it's okay. You see, I'd lost all hope, thought my life was over, but then, Marcus was there, and I knew I was saved. From the first moment I saw his face, I knew he would rescue me. I was right. Omar and his men were trying to take me to their leader. They called him their benefactor. Marcus's team tracked us and during the drive to the airport in Moldova, Omar tried to...," she sucked in a deep breath, "he tried to rape me."

"That bastard!" Jasmin hugged Fatima tighter. "I'm so sorry!"

"He didn't succeed. Marcus and his team stopped him. He saved my life."

Pride filled Jasmin's heart. She was proud of her big brother, but never more so than upon hearing Fatima's tale. "That's Marcus. Helping folks is what he's always done. I guess that's why he joined the military. It's why he taught me how to shoot, that's for sure. He's looked out for me all my life."

Fatima smiled. "He's a good brother, and a good son," she said, sliding a look at his mother napping in the big blue chair.

Mrs. DuBose snuffled, smacking her lips, and mumbled, "We locked the door, didn't we?"

"What door, mama?" Jasmin asked.

"The basement, sugar. But that old root cellar is a hot mess. Need to clean out those boxes," she said, eyes fluttering closed again.

Jasmin made a face. "I cleaned out those boxes a month ago. Mama's getting a bit forgetful."

"You have a root cellar?" Fatima asked.

"Yeah, but we don't use it. It's an old house. Marcus put a lock on the outside doors last time he was here. Should still be secured outside even if the hall door is open. Doesn't matter since we're surrounded by soldiers. No one's gonna get past them." She patted Fatima's shoulder. "Don't worry."

Sliding an arm around Jasmin's waist, she returned the hug. "I'm not worried. Your brother will not let anything happen to us."

Jasmin noted the complete trust in Fatima's eyes as she spoke of her big brother. She suppressed a smile and nodded in agreement. Together, they held vigil watching the bedroom door and listening closely to the eerie silence in the house.

Chapter 10

From his perch on a tree branch in the backyard, Skyscraper noted the lamplight still glowing inside his old bedroom. He'd climbed up the sturdy oak via the worn wooden boards nailed into the trunk in a ladder pattern. These, he'd added himself when he was but a boy. Back then, the tree was less thick and the branch that jutted out over the backyard near the fence line was smaller. He'd been much smaller as well not yet having hit the growth spurt that sent him well over six and a half feet tall. The branch afforded him the best possible vantage point from which to surveil the back of the house. Spanish moss hanging like elegant lace amid the green leaves helped hide him from view to anyone on the ground. Crouched like a tiger on an adjacent branch was Outlaw. He stayed nearer the trunk of the tree, not as trusting of his branch as Skyscraper who stretched out on his belly like a deadly python.

At the front of the house, Badger kept watch hidden behind their SUV parked against the curb. Next to him, Jersey peered out from the bumper, his eyes searching the darkness on his side of N. Roman Street. Hollywood guarded the east entry to the street from a ditch while Ghost maintained his choke point on the west end from atop the roof of an empty house. Each was armed with the weapons Hollywood procured earlier. Each was camouflaged to blend into the darkness from their dark attire to the black knit caps on their heads and the black smudge sticks applied to their faces to hide their skin. As soldiers, they were terrifying to behold.

Skyscraper knew there was no way anyone would get past his team without getting caught. The moment Omar Baz and the two Muhammeds showed their faces, they would be ensnared, and the two non-essential terrorists quickly dispatched. The plan was simple. Let them walk into the trap and then close the escape routes from behind. Bowie knives would quietly end the first two obstacles. Their bodies would be moved to the trunk of the Suburban. Baz would be taken down non-lethally, sedated, gagged, and tied. All three would be taken from the scene at that point. A quick call to their only secure contact at this time would send the cavalry in to collect Omar. Afterwards, he and his team would handle disposing of the two bodies. Mission accomplished and Fatima and his family would be safe.

As plans go, it was good. But he knew too well that oft-times, plans went awry. Despite the quiet of the night, he felt uneasy, and he didn't like it. For one, they had no idea where Baz was in New Orleans, had no way to track him. And with a mole inside command, their only safe contact was retired Navy SEAL, Jesse 'Rio' Taggart. Retired was a loose term since Rio still served. It was understood that Rio, following an injury which took over a year to heal, had graduated from the field to intelligence. The man was a computer genius. There was no one he couldn't track down. No information he couldn't uncover. Except where the hell their teammate Eastwood was being rehabilitated after having half his leg blown off in Kuwait. Outlaw had asked, but Rio didn't seem to know. All he'd shared was that Doc had asked the same question. There was also a cryptic message to Doc via Mrs. Tyler, Eastwood's mom. He'd told her to tell Doc *"Dig a little deeper"* and *"tell him I ain't dead, just a broke dick."* Rio said he was working on it. Still, it didn't make sense when a few taps of the computer keyboard usually wielded answers immediately. Something was up, but now wasn't the time. Skyscraper's mind ran the gamut from Baz to the mole to their missing brother in arms. It only added to his mental unrest.

"I can hear your hamster wheel spinning all the way over here, Marcus."

His commander didn't normally call him by his first name. Skyscraper knew his uneasiness must be spooking his captain. "Sorry, Outlaw," he whispered. "Just thinking."

"About?"

A sigh escaped his lips as Skyscraper scanned the backyard. "Too much shit. Like what to do about Fatima."

This surprised Outlaw. His eyebrow hitched as he bit his lip to keep from laughing. Skyscraper had been completely out of sorts since he'd first laid eyes on the young woman. Having gone through a similar life-changing experience in London, he could sympathize. Meeting Emma had changed everything in his life—for the better—but he'd gone through his own personal hell first before arriving in the realm of wedded bliss.

"It's simple, Sky. You kill two terrorists. Bag one. Deliver the girl and Omar Baz to D.C., and then, it's over." From his perch, Outlaw saw Skyscraper's shoulders stiffen. He couldn't see the man's face, but he knew without a doubt Marcus's expression was a comical combination of acceptance of the mission parameters and rejection of this assessment.

"That's not what I meant." The quiet words held an angry edge.

Laughter threatened to spill from Outlaw's lips, but he swallowed it down. "No? Then what, pray tell, is the problem? Has the girl given you any difficulty? Say the word and I'll have Hollywood take over watching her."

"What? No!" Skyscraper threw a furious look over his shoulder, nearly falling off his branch. He hung on, but continued, "Don't even think of letting that hormonal hound dog near her! If he touches her, I'll cut off his damned fingers and feed them to him like Snausages."

The reference to doggie snacks did him in. Outlaw snorted, laughter bubbling up.

"Captain?" Skyscraper looked at his commander like he'd grown another head.

"Sorry," Outlaw chuckled, getting himself under control and lowering his voice once again. "I was fucking with you, Marcus. Damn, man, it's obvious you're smitten. Everyone sees it."

Skyscraper didn't like hearing this. "It's no one's damned business," he said, facing the backyard once again.

"It's the team's business," said Outlaw, "but only if it interferes with the mission. You've never let me down,

Sky, and I don't expect you'll begin now no matter how beautiful the girl. The plan is the plan. We terminate two non-essentials. Bag Baz, and we deliver both him and Fatima Ali to D.C. That's how it has to be." He noticed Skyscraper's shoulders slump. "But after that, after the State Department debriefs her and does what they need to do, you might just have a chance. Who knows?"

Skyscraper's head came up. "You think so? Think she'd give me a chance?"

Outlaw reached out and gave Skyscraper's foot a friendly shake. "Why not? You're a good man. You deserve happiness."

A grin spread across Marcus's face. Compliments from his Captain usually came in the form of "Nice kill, Skyscraper." Nate saying he was a good man, despite some of the haunting things he'd done and still would do as a soldier meant a lot to him. If Outlaw and Doc could find love, then why not himself? Hope washed over him like a balm to his battered soul. "Thanks, Captain."

"Anytime—"

A loud scream ripped through the night followed by a barrage of gunshots.

"What the fuck?" Skyscraper jumped down from his branch, Outlaw hot on his heels. Both men ran to the house, one of them more terrified than he'd ever been in his life.

Chapter 11

Skyscraper kicked in the back door and went in hot, the barrel of his AR-15 leading the way. He sighted left to the bedroom door and found his mother standing there, the Winchester still smoking.

"Mama, what happened? Where's Fatima? Where's Jasmin?"

"That way!" she shouted, pointing down the hall. "It's all my fault. I knew I didn't lock that door."

"What door, Mrs. Dubose?" Outlaw asked.

"The root cellar. I just knew it, but I fell asleep. When I woke up, two men were here. They got our girls. Marcus, you have to go get them before they get away!"

"Shit!" Skyscraper touched his mother's shoulder. "You okay?"

"I'm fine. Just go!" Magnolia DuBose slapped her son's hand away, tears filling her brown eyes. "Oh, dear Lord."

"Stay in my room. Barricade the door." Skyscraper ran down the hall and turned the corner. The door to the root cellar was wide open and the hallway smelled of butane. A black mark showed the impact from what appeared to be a flash-bang, but it made no sense that one would be deployed by the terrorists.

Outlaw quickly provided an answer. "Looks like our bombmaker has been busy. Homemade flash-bang. Didn't work, though." He pulled out his two-way radio. "Ghost, Badger, come in."

The radio sputtered as Outlaw and Skyscraper descended the stairs, aiming as they went.

"Ghost here, Six. Come back."

"Keep sharp," Outlaw whispered, "the enemy was inside the house. I repeat, they were inside the house. God-damned root cellar. Must've reconned it before we arrived. They have Fatima and Jasmin. Close the net, men."

At the foot of the stairs, Skyscraper saw signs of struggle. Gardening tools that hung on the wall were strewn about the floor and the outer cellar doors were thrown wide. As he and Outlaw ascended the steps, gaining the side yard, a scream reached their ears.

Skyscraper looked towards the front of the house. He ran to the sound. Coming from beneath the low-hanging branches of the large magnolia tree were two men. One had Jasmin who was kicking and biting, clearly pissed off, but the large man holding her in a bear hug raised his hand, striking her hard across the face.

"Get your fucking hands off my sister, motherfucker!" Skyscraper ran forward, Outlaw at his back.

The big man raised a hand to Jasmin's neck. In it was a syringe, the needle no more than an inch from pricking her skin.

"Back off or I kill her here," he said, speaking Arabic.

Recognizing his words, Skyscraper slowed his pace, but continued to stalk him. Behind the man he now determined was Muhammed Daher Tahan stood Omar Baz. He remembered him well from Old Town Bucharest. Baz had Fatima in a headlock, a gun pressed to her temple. There was panic in her eyes, but her demeanor was calm, as if she were fighting to remain in control. Her bravery made his heart swell, but her predicament filled him with horror. He'd never felt fear before in dealing with terrorists, but then, he'd never before had anything to lose. Neither of the two men would hesitate to kill Jasmin, but Fatima, they needed. He had to tread carefully.

Keeping his eyes on Fatima, he spoke, choosing his words with caution. "It's going to be okay." To Daher Tahan, he said, "If you harm my sister, there is nothing in this life that will save you. I'll slice you up myself, piece by piece, and feed your sorry carcass to the gators.

"Big talk from a big man," said Baz, who then spoke in rapid Arabic to Daher Tahan.

The man blinked, eyeing Skyscraper, and he knew Baz had translated his words. The two continued backing up moving toward the road.

Outlaw followed their line of sight to a black Highlander parked in the driveway across the way one house down. They hadn't noticed it since it wasn't on the street. The second Muhammed sat in the driver's seat, the engine on. The Highlander was facing out, ready to drive off into the night. They couldn't let that happen. He caught Badger's eye peeking around the front bumper of their stolen Suburban. Miraculously, a crop of blue hydrangeas about four feet tall sprawled at the edge of the lawn across the street hid his men from the getaway driver's view.

Badger signaled Jersey who set off hunkered down low, practically doing a belly-crawl across the pavement until he could skirt around the large flowering bush. Badger moved around the bumper and positioned himself, aiming his AR-15.

Skyscraper took another step. "This big man is going to hurt you like you've never been hurt before, Omar." Baz blinked. "That's right. I know who you are, and I know who you work for. Prince Nayef isn't going to be happy with you. You go back empty-handed, he's going to kill you. Slowly."

"Who says I'm going back empty-handed?" he asked, backing one foot off the curb. "I have my prize. The prince will reward me with great riches, moneys I will spend training my brothers to kill all of you infidels." His eyes narrowed as he pulled Fatima closer, tightening his hold. "And he will give me that which I desire to do with as I please."

Struggling to breathe with Omar's arm wrapped around her neck, Fatima reached into her pocket. The flash-bang inside the house failed. Temporarily blinded and ears ringing, she'd tried to make a run for it. But Daher Tahan still had Jasmin and she couldn't leave her. It was that hesitation which allowed Omar to capture her once again. He narrowly escaped the shots fired by Mrs. DuBose. His anger at the old woman scared her so much she ran towards Jasmin knowing he would follow. It didn't stop her from attempting to free Marcus's sister. She scratched at Daher Tahan's eyes while Jasmin kicked and punched. Jasmin tried reaching for her Sig, but the gun had come loose in the scuffle and lay on the floor out of reach.

When Omar's arms grabbed her and pulled her down the stairs, she knew they were in trouble. Now, she had one more chance. The homemade taser rested in her palm, still inside the pocket of her skirt. She turned it on, carefully pulling it out. It would take a moment to charge fully, but if Marcus kept Omar talking, she'd have a chance to take him down.

Skyscraper kept his eyes on both Baz and Daher Tahan. The immediate threat was to his sister. He needed to neutralize the man before he plunged that needle into Jasmin's neck. He had no idea what was in the syringe, and he didn't want to find out the hard way. He caught Badger out of his peripheral vision noting he was in position, ready to make a kill shot. Ghost and Hollywood would be closing in fast from the ends of N. Roman Street. He couldn't see him, but he knew Jersey would be on the second Muhammed. He hadn't spotted Jersey yet, but he'd bet good money Outlaw had since he'd gone quiet. A quiet Outlaw was a deadly, plotting Outlaw.

To his left, a dark figure emerged from the side fence, creeping slowly with a slight limp. The sound of a bolt being loaded into a chamber met his ears.

"This the problem we've been expectin'?"

"Mr. Emmet, go back into the house. Now, please!" Seeing the old man with his rifle raised and ready to fire sent panic shooting down Skyscraper's spine. First Fatima and Jasmin, and now Mr. Emmet. That was too many people he cared about, all in danger, and all because of him. All because he failed to double-check the root cellar.

"What's this? Old men and women fighting your battles?" Omar took two more steps into the street jerking Fatima along. Daher Tahan yanked Jasmin's hair forcing her neck at a painful angle.

"You bastard!" she yelled, sending an elbow into the big man's ribs. He grunted but held tighter.

"Let her go!" Skyscraper marched forward with menace. "Jas, don't worry. I'm gonna kill this sonofabitch."

"Not if I kill him first," she grunted, panting for breath.

Her snark made him smile. As long as she was talking, he could keep the two terrorists distracted long enough to find his moment.

"Remember what I taught you, Marcus," said Emmet.

"Stay focused and keep God in my heart," Skyscraper replied.

"Amen, son. Now let's handle this business." Mr. Emmet stepped forward once, planted his foot, exhaled, and fired.

The syringe in Daher Tahan's hand exploded along with his hand. Bits of skin and bone flew as blood sprayed in all directions.

Marcus ran full-tilt at Daher Tahan, slamming the butt of his rifle into the man's face. He dropped like a sack of potatoes. Jasmin twisted away, rolling to the ground where Outlaw reached for her, pulling her to her feet and away from the fight. She looked around for Fatima and saw the other man who'd dragged them violently from her brother's room pulling her across the street.

In the chaos, Fatima saw her chance. She was about to jam the taser into his ribs when Jasmin yelled, panicked.

"No! You're not clear of his body. It'll take you down too!"

Baz looked down and saw her contrived weapon. Fury contorted his face. He slammed a fist on her arm knocking the taser free of her hand. Then he let loose her neck and snaked his arm around her waist, bodily lifting her as he ran for the Highlander. Inside the vehicle, Muhammed bin Salib rolled down his window, stuck out his hand and took aim. He fired off a volley of bullets as Omar reached the passenger door shoving Fatima inside before climbing in next to her.

Salib put the Highlander in gear ready to take off. His attention was split between shooting at the Americans and following Baz's orders.

"Go! Forget Daher Tahan! Get out of here! Eajal! Eajal!" '*Hurry*' he shouted in Arabic

Salib glanced at Baz. Anger sparked as he furiously followed the order to leave his brother behind, his foot coming off the brake. He opened his mouth to protest, but his words were abruptly cut off. A bullet slammed into his head silencing the man forever. The SUV rolled forward. Standing on the driver's side, Jersey reached for the door handle.

Baz opened his door and grabbed Fatima's arm in a tight grip using her as a shield. He pulled them both out of the rolling vehicle taking off in a full-out run between two houses, ducking through bushes and dragging the woman behind him to the open alley.

Then all hell broke loose.

Chapter 12

U p and down the block, lights came on. The residents of N. Roman Street had heard the gunfire. This was bad for the team.

Skyscraper spat on the ground breathing hard. He'd hauled off and punched Daher Tahan in the face three times rendering the man unconscious. He turned to Badger who'd come rushing across the street. "Take this one! You know what to do," he said.

"Baz has Fatima. Jersey has their tail. I got this one. Go."

Skyscraper picked up his rifle and headed across the street. Something made him turn around. His eyes scanned the lawn. Outlaw had Jasmin, Badger had the first Muhammed. Ghost was crouched over someone lying on the ground.

It was Mr. Emmet.

"No!" The cry ripped from Marcus's lips. Mrs. Emmet came running from next door and his mother made her way down the front steps.

"Call 9-1-1!" Mrs. Emmet howled, dropping to her knees next to her husband.

His mother caught his eye. "Go, Marcus! Don't let him get away. Get her! We got this!"

Hollywood ran up stopping short at his side. "Go. I'll follow in the Suburban."

Skyscraper tamped down his rage. Omar had Fatima again, something he promised would not happen. His mother's house had been invaded by terrorists, and now, Mr. Emmet might be dead. Fury fueled him as a deadly calm took over. He turned and ran between the two houses following in Jersey's footsteps. He had to catch up. No one would deal with Baz but him, and in this moment, he wasn't sure he'd be able to follow orders. Baz didn't deserve to live. He reminded himself that accidents happened in the field all the time.

Behind him, Outlaw went into damage control mode.

"Badger, you and Ghost get sleeping beauty off the lawn now!" He turned to Mrs. DuBose. "I hate to ask, but—"

She turned, and without batting an eye, said, "The root cellar. Tie 'em up and lock them in. Quick, before the police get here."

Outlaw cleared his throat. "Pretty sure one of them is dead, ma'am." The statement was more a way of questioning whether Skyscraper's mom was really okay with him commandeering a corner of her house as a makeshift holding cell, at least until the police came and went. He also didn't like Skyscraper going after Omar alone. In his current state of mind, he would filet Baz for taking Fatima and nearly abducting his sister.

"A bullet to the head will do that. Why you wastin' time, Captain? Move!" The tough-as-nails woman planted her hands on her hips, her face filled with a familiar motherly annoyance.

"Yes, ma'am!" He didn't need to be told a third time. Twice was enough. "Ghost, the root cellar. I'll get the dead weight." Ghost and Badger had already hog-tied Daher Tahan who was still unconscious, his wound where his hand used to be bleeding all over the lawn.

"I have some duct tape in the garage," said Mrs. DuBose. "Jas, go get it for them. They'll need to make sure that one stays quiet in case he wakes up."

Ghost nodded. "Perfect. Thanks." He and Badger worked together quickly lifting the unconscious man and carrying him to the side of the house and down the stairs. Once they reached the bottom of the stairs, they picked a far corner and deposited the unconscious terrorist. Jasmin joined them, handing over the roll of duct tape and some extra rope.

"In case you need more." She watched as Badger wrapped the tape around the man's mouth going around his head twice to secure it. Then, he taped up the bloody stump, and linked the extra rope through the ties around Daher Tahan's wrists and ankles before attaching the other end to a hook hanging from the ceiling.

A loud thump startled Jasmin who turned to find a dead body rolling to a stop at her feet. The captain came down the stairs after it. Upon seeing Marcus's sister, he cleared his throat. "Sorry, I didn't know you were down here."

She stared in horror at the corpse. Half his face was blown off, a bloody, matted mess.

"I hate to ask, but would it be possible to borrow your car?"

Jasmin heard his words but couldn't tear her eyes away from the dead terrorist, although she desperately wanted to. A sick feeling pooled in the pit of her stomach.

Badger came up behind her, gently turning her around. "Ma'am," he said, his voice soft, "We should get you out of here. Come with me," he said, leading her up the stairs and keeping himself between her and the body. "The captain would like to know if we could borrow your car. We need to go help your brother."

"I've never seen a dead person before," she whispered.

Badger gave her shoulder a comforting squeeze as they gained the yard once again. Outlaw and Ghost followed. "You did well. Most people would really freak out. I'm proud of you, Jasmin. You're tough like your brother. We need to leave them down there until the police and ambulance have come and gone."

Behind him, Outlaw and Ghost closed the double doors of the root cellar. Ghost shoved the handle of a short garden shovel he'd picked up on the way out through the door handles.

"You'll need to go inside and lock the interior door. Don't go down there for any reason. We'll take care of this just as soon as we can." Outlaw stood watching Jasmin. Shock was setting in fast now.

Shaking herself, she sucked in a breath. "You need to borrow my car." She reached into her jeans pocket and pulled out a set of keys. "It's the dark blue Impala," she said.

Outlaw knew this already having determined the car parked behind Mrs. DuBose's old Ford truck would be her daughter's. "We'll be careful with it. And thank you."

Badger shared a look with Outlaw. "I can stay with her, handle the situation here."

"That's a good idea."

Ghost nodded in agreement. "Just in case the police get nosy."

Jasmin looked at her mother. The old woman was on her knees next to Mrs. Emmet. A few neighbors had come out to join them. In the distance, and ambulance siren could be heard. "My car will be in the way. The ambulance won't be able to get in. Give me the keys. I'll move it down the street. Captain, you slip out the side so no one sees you. Take the car from there."

Badger looked impressed. "Damn, you really are as tough as Skyscraper."

"It runs in the family," she said. "Doesn't mean I like it." She turned to leave and stopped, glancing over her shoulder. "I'll tell them it was a drive-by. Gang violence. Probably initiation. Happens all the time 'round these parts." She took off, running across the lawn pausing only to tell her mother that she needed to move the car so the ambulance could get in.

Outlaw heard Mrs. DuBose reply, "Good idea, Jas." She looked back over her shoulder nodding her head once before returning her focus to her friends and neighbors.

"After you secure and hide that Highlander in the street, get inside, Badger. Use the backdoor, and make sure that interior cellar door is closed and locked. You can keep me apprised on the walkie." Outlaw tapped Ghost and the two of them ducked low moving along the fence line before dropping behind some bushes. They emerged on the street two houses down. There, they met up with Jasmin and took the car. The young woman jogged back to her mother's house, rejoining the scene. No one noticed them taking off. Everyone turned to the bright, flashing red lights of the ambulance approaching from the opposite end of N. Roman Street.

Inside the Impala, Outlaw hailed Hollywood on his two-way radio. "Come in, Hollywood. What's your location?"

Static sputtered over the channel, and then, "*Catching up to Skyscraper two miles north. I had no idea he could run this fast. I swear, he's like a cheetah. Target has entered a warehouse. I'm closing in. Over.*"

"Send the address to my cell. We're on our way. Don't let Skyscraper do anything stupid. That's an order! Six out."

❧❧❧❧❧ ❧❧❧❧❧

Fatima struggled to stay upright. Omar had a death-grip on her wrist. It was going to leave a mark. Another one. Just when she thought she would never have to face this monster again he'd snatched her from the safety of Marcus's bedroom. She and Jasmin shared the small twin bed, talking softly for a while. The sound of Mrs. Dubose's light snoring was an odd comfort and having both her and Jasmin near lulled her into a false sense of security. Fatigue long denied rolled over her like a warm wave pulling her under. She felt safe in the knowledge that Marcus and his men surrounded the house. No one would get in.

Then, brutal hands grabbed her and covered her mouth. She was pulled roughly from the mattress and before she could squeak out a warning, a second man grabbed Jasmin. Fatima kicked and threw her elbows trying to break Omar's all-to-familiar hold. Panic flooded her body and grew stronger when she saw the second man, one she did not recognize, kick the recliner over with Mrs. DuBose still in it. The old woman hit the ground hard, the chair rolling on top of her.

She and Jasmin were hauled out of the room while Mrs. DuBose struggled to push the chair off. The men carried them down the hall as she and Jasmin fought to break free. The sound of a shotgun startled her. Omar ducked, his hand moving from her mouth to instinctively cover his own head. That's when she screamed and deployed her makeshift flash-bang. It went off, further startling everyone. Smoke filled the hallway but dispersed quickly.

Beside her, Jasmin's foot kicked at the wall throwing her abductor off balance. They fell and Jasmin broke away, but the man grabbed her ankle and pulled her back. Fatima ran to Jasmin to help but Omar clamped his hand over her mouth again and dragged her down the stairs into the root cellar. That's when Fatima realized Omar had been inside the house the entire time. This horrifying realization made her sick. Worse than knowing he was inside, was knowing Marcus was outside and he and his team had no idea what was going on.

She did what she could to slow Omar down making as much noise as possible. Marcus would save them. He'd promised!

She nearly fainted with fear when Mr. Emmet took a bullet. She saw the man go down. And then Omar's driver died before her eyes. She thought for sure it was over then. Marcus's teammate, Jersey was there, mere steps away, but Omar pulled her from the SUV, sheer menace riddling his pock-marked face, and forced her to run under threat of his gun. If she balked now, there would be nothing left of her for Marcus to rescue. She knew Omar was serious. With so many soldiers after him, one of his men dead, and the other captured, he had nothing left to lose.

Now they were entering a large warehouse. It was dark and uninhabited. Omar stopped briefly, firing a shot into the padlock on the back door. It shattered, allowing him entry. He dragged her through behind him, then turned and pulled the door closed.

The old metal building housed a variety of parade floats. Some had large Joker heads and others, outsized papier-maché animals with bizarre, macabre expressions. The whole place felt like a child's nightmare come to life. A rat scurried past, and she bit back a scream.

"Come!" Omar's grip tightened on her arm.

"Omar, stop!" She dug in her heels.

Baz looked at her like she'd lost her mind. "You dare? Move or I'll kill you here and now!"

Fatima pulled back from him. The move caused instant fury as she knew it would. "Do it then. Kill me," she taunted.

He moved close, bringing his face within an inch of her own. "Death is too good for you, Fatima. I have other plans." He licked his lips, his angry eyes roving over her face and down her body.

Fatima felt his gaze as he ogled her. It was vile, and she felt violated. She swallowed the bile that threatened to rise and pulled away as much as she could. She knew then that no matter his threats, Omar wouldn't kill her. For one, his Saudi prince benefactor would put out a hit on him. He knew it, but it wasn't fear of his own death that drove him, it was his own sick lust. He wanted her. Wanted to defile her, to abuse her, all for his own sadistic satisfaction and gross gratification.

But she knew something he didn't. Something he wasn't taking seriously. Marcus was coming for her. She knew Jersey had followed. She saw him run after them with her own eyes, but then he'd dropped from view, whether by accident or design, she didn't know. Even so, where one of them went, they all followed, and Marcus promised to keep her safe. He was a man of his word. This was something she'd already discovered about him. He protected the people he cared about. Oddly, she dared to include herself among this privileged circle of individuals. The way he'd treated her from the first moment their eyes met confirmed this. And then there were his kisses. She blushed recalling the feel of his lips on hers, his hands caressing her body, and the evidence of his desire pressing firmly against her womanly core.

Omar noticed the pinkening in her cheeks, mistaking its cause. A sinister smile pulled at the edges of his thin lips.

"I see you like the idea too." He reached around, pulling her fully against his body. "I knew you would. I've dreamed often of what I will do to you, Fatima. Once the prince gives you to me..."

She felt his hands grope her backside, the hard metal of the gun pressing into her tailbone. She pushed hard at his chest, turning her face away as his lips sought hers. He found her ear instead.

Omar panted, grinding his hips as his tongue shot out, licking her lobe before biting it hard.

"Ow!" She struggled, desperately trying to slam her knee into his groin. "You are gross, Omar! I would never consider you, do you hear me?"

"You will not have a choice. Maybe I should show you now," he said, looking around the warehouse as he lifted her bodily, carrying her swiftly to a parade float flatbed. He threw her down, stunning her momentarily.

Fatima felt her head hit the flatbed, her ears ringing. Omar was poised above her, fury and lust in his eyes. Pulling up her knees, she placed her feet on his chest as he descended upon her and kicked with all her might. Caught off guard, Omar flew back falling hard onto the concrete floor.

Fatima rolled to her left and jumped off the flatbed, running away. She made a hard-right dashing down a row between giant floats. Behind her, Omar howled, furious.

"Bitch! I'm going to kill you for sure, but first, you will know what hell truly is, Christian! I'm going to violate every orifice in your body until you bleed!"

Fear snaked through Fatima as she ran. The warehouse was large, but she knew she was heading to the opposite side. She only hoped there was a door leading out. There had to be!

Adrenaline pumped through her as she zigged, then zagged down long rows. She was nearing the far side, could see the wall as she drew closer. Her lungs burned. She glanced over her shoulder, terrified Omar was gaining on her.

A hand clamped over her mouth, and she was lifted off her feet. Her heart raced. Panicking, she kicked, fighting to break free.

"Sssh! It's me, Fatima," a low voice whispered in her ear.

She froze. She knew the voice, knew the hands holding her. Marcus had come for her. She twisted around, gripping his waist and pressing her face to his chest.

Skyscraper wrapped his arms around her protectively. He could feel her shaking, but her voice was steady as she spoke softly, catching her breath.

"We must stop him, Marcus. He won't quit coming after me." Fatima raised her hand to her face, unconsciously rubbing her cheek.

Skyscraper felt his blood run cold. As carefully as he could manage, he touched the skin of her wrist. It was bruised a bright purple so fresh he could see it in the dim light of the dark warehouse. He held her fingers and pushed up her sleeve. More bruising met his inquiring gaze.

"He did this to you?" His eyes held hers, his tone deceptively neutral.

Fatima pulled her hand from his. She nodded. "I'm okay. Really. I've survived worse."

Skyscraper saw red. With a hard-fought calmness, he asked, "What else has he done to you?"

His quiet words didn't fool her. "It's not important anymore. What's important is stopping him."

"Tell me, Fatima," he insisted. Skyscraper gentled his voice and cupped her face in his large hands. "Please."

She could see he would not be put off and time was not on their side. "He has beat me, burned me with cigarettes, and twice now tried to rape me. He says the prince will give me to him and he is determined to have his way."

Her courage amazed him. Pulling her deeper into the space between two massive floats decorated in harlequin motifs, he cradled her head, his thumbs caressing her cheeks. "I'm sorry this happened. I failed you. I won't fail again." With that, he dropped a soft kiss on her lips. "Stay low," he said, pointing at the underside of the float's flatbed. "Hide there. I'll come for you when it's over. Don't come out for anyone—"

"Except you," she whispered, nodding.

Skyscraper smiled.

Fatima ducked down, fitting her body under the small space, and edging around a tire. Peeking out, her eyes found his. "Marcus, be careful."

Her words touched him but his fury towards Omar was red-hot. "Don't worry," he said, "this isn't my first time."

He waited for her to retreat all the way beneath the float. When he couldn't see her anymore, he got low and checked the aisle. Glancing up, he caught sight of Jersey. Perrillo had climbed up to a second-floor walkway that led to a small office in the corner. He gave Skyscraper a thumbs-up as he held his position, rifle aiming over the metal railing. Evaluating the layout, he ran the possibilities through his head like he'd done on hundreds of missions before. Outside, Hollywood was surely already gaining entry just as Jersey had done. Quietly, giving nothing away. That's how they rolled. Most likely his teammate had located every point of entry and would seek the best vantage point to cover all. If there wasn't a single vantage point, which Skyscraper concluded was the case, then Hollywood would cut off all but one point of entry. This would be the one located away from prying eyes. A back door.

He eyed the stairs Jersey climbed to reach the upper walkway. At the foot was a door clearly marked exit, but it was on the backside of the building. Not the obvious entry.

He'd come in behind Omar at the main entrance. That meant that door was now cut off. Omar wouldn't know that. It would be the first place he'd run if he was smart enough to run. Without a doubt, Skyscraper knew the terrorist was beyond acting intelligently at this point. He was desperate, and a desperate man was an unpredictable and dangerous foe. He would have to lure Omar out into the open. With Jersey as his lookout, he moved into the aisle, keeping his head low.

Two rows down he reached into his pocket and pulled out a handful of coins. One by one, he threw them towards a clearing in the center of the warehouse. The sound of the first two hitting the concrete floor and rolling to a stop was loud in the silence. Skyscraper listened intently; his semi-automatic rifle aimed out as his eyes scanned the rows. His patience paid off.

A single footfall followed by the soft sound of a frustrated breath being expelled met his trained ear. And then...

"Fatima, you know I will find you again," he said. Omar was taunting her. Stalking her. Unaware he, too, was being stalked. "You will be mine, and when I find you, I'm going to punish you for wasting my time. Your soldier friends cannot save you. Their days are numbered. My benefactor is seeing to it. No one is going to help you. You. Are..." Omar paused, the rubber soles of his shoes coming to a stop as he came to the edge of the opening. "Mine!" He stepped out, sighting left and right with his handgun, his eyes searching the open space. Finding it empty, he shouted, "Bitch! I promise you, Fatima, you are going to wish for death long before it finds you."

Skyscraper moved like a python; his muscles used to shrinking his 6'7" frame down in order to sneak up on the enemy. From his peripheral vision he noted Jersey sighting Omar. As he drew closer, coming up on Omar's flank, Baz froze. Skyscraper stopped, watchful.

Omar was looking at something on the ground. He squatted down, reaching out to pick it up. He eyed the quarter in his hand. Suddenly, he swung around, arms raised, handgun aimed, firing.

Skyscraper rolled right, the bullet zinging past his ear. He came up, rifle raised pulling the trigger twice. Two short bursts found their marks, one in Omar's left shoulder, the other lodging in his left side breaking ribs. Baz went down clutching his shoulder, a stunned expression on his face. Coming closer, Skyscraper eyed the man.

Baz still clutched the handgun in his right hand, his left hand pressing against the bleeding hole in his side.

"You think you've won, soldier-boy?" he said, sneering. "She will never be free. My benefactor will have her, one way or the other."

Skyscraper's eyes narrowed. He watched as the blood loss weakened the terrorist. His skin grew paler, and his hand shook as he tried to take aim at the towering Green Beret standing over him. With a well-aimed kick, Skyscraper sent the handgun flying from Omar's grip. He pointed the AR-15 at Baz's head. "No, he won't. And neither will you, you rapist sonofabitch."

Skyscraper's finger tightened on the trigger, squeezing.

"Stand down, Sergeant!"

Outlaw ran in behind him, the order flying from his lips.

When Skyscraper hesitated, Outlaw yelled, "That's an order, Marcus!"

Coming up behind him, the captain grabbed the rifle pushing it out and away. Behind him, Hollywood and Ghost rushed in surrounding Omar Baz covering the target.

Still poised to strike, Skyscraper inhaled. "He tried to rape her, captain. Again!"

Outlaw threw a look of disgust at Baz. "I understand, Marcus, but we have orders to bring him in." Outlaw nodded at Ghost who moved to secure Baz's wrists. Once the zip-ties were in place, he pulled out a First Aid kit and went to work staunching the bleeding from the gunshot wounds. "Jersey, I know you're up there. Get down here and cover this miserable fuck. Hollywood, call Rio and give him our location. Tell him to send in the cavalry. We need transport out ASAP."

"Roger that, Captain."

Outlaw gently pulled Skyscraper away. "Where's the girl? Where's Fatima?"

At the mention of her name, Skyscraper blinked and then turned, focusing on Outlaw. "She's safe. I'll get her."

"Go, then. We need to be ready."

Skyscraper threw one last look at Baz who was now laid out on his non-injured side being tended by Ghost. He didn't deserve to live. "One day, Baz, I'm going to send you straight to hell."

Omar gasped and laughed through the pain. "But not today, soldier-boy. Know this, I do not fear death. Allah waits for me, his loyal son."

"Hellfire awaits you, you sick fuck. There's no paradise where you're going." A sinister half-smile tugged at Skyscraper's lips. He pointed a finger at Omar Baz mimicking a gun and said, "Bang, motherfucker. Count on it."

Chapter 13

The hours following the takedown at the warehouse were exhausting, but Fatima would not trade them for all the money in the world. Knowing Omar Baz had been taken into custody by the military and FBI removed a weight from her shoulders she didn't know she'd been carrying. There was also the flight from New Orleans to D.C., first by helicopter that took them from a field opposite the warehouse to the Naval Air Station Joint Reserve Base. There, they boarded a transport to Washington, D. C. During both flights, Marcus stayed by her side, his hand holding hers the entire time. She'd never felt safer than she did next to this man.

Jersey stayed behind to rejoin Badger while the captain, Ghost, and Hollywood flew with them. When she asked why the two other men did not come along, Marcus offered a cryptic reply.

"They have a little bit of cleaning up to do."

She assumed that meant Omar's flunkies and probably speaking with authorities.

"And what will happen next?" She looked into his eyes.

Skyscraper exhaled, relaxing for the first time in days. "Well, you're going to be reunited with your mom, for one thing," he said.

Fatima smiled, snuggling closer into his side. "I can't wait to see her. I've missed her so much."

"She's missed you too. You're tough like her, you know that?"

"I am not tough, as you say. I've simply tried to survive."

Her humble reply left him nearly speechless. Reaching out, he lifted her chin. "Listen to me, Fatima. What you've accomplished under the worst of circumstances is nothing less than a damned miracle. When most people would've given up, given in, you fought, and you lived. You're stronger than you realize, and I think you're amazing."

She was struck by the sincerity of his words. "Thank you." She could think of no other reply. "I think you're amazing too, Marcus." She smiled, covering his fingers with her own. "You're my very own knight in shining armor. My hero. Before you, I thought only of my father as a hero. He always loved us, protected us, even to his dying breath. I didn't think anyone else would ever make me feel safe, but you have. I didn't think anyone could make me believe in such fairy tale notions, but you have, Marcus. I know it's silly. Really, I do, but..." she paused, searching for the right words.

"What?"

She swallowed. "You make me believe again in the goodness of others. That's a miracle in and of itself, and I lo—"

"Attention," came a voice in the cockpit, "This is Captain Buchwald, we'll be landing in thirty minutes. Please remain in your seats and keep your seatbelts fastened until we've come to a complete stop at the terminal."

"Time to put this back on," Skyscraper said, reaching over to re-buckle her seatbelt. After making sure she was settled, he did the same. Then, leaning over, he kissed her cheek just shy of her lips and whispered, "I'm glad I make you feel safe."

A blush crept up her neck and heat flushed her body.

Skyscraper noticed and his eyes gleamed. "The military higher ups and the State Department are going to take you for questioning. Don't be afraid. Tell them everything. I'm sure your mom will be close by to keep you company."

"And where will you be?" She sounded anxious.

"I have some debriefing to do. Not sure how long it will take." He stroked her fingers absently.

"But when will I see you again?"

He smiled. "Do you want to see me again?"

"I...yes."

"I can't say for sure, Fatima. It will depend on a lot of things, but I promise you this," he said, lifting her hand to his lips and kissing her fingertips. "I'll find you."

"But how," she insisted. "You won't know where I will be. I have no phone, no address right now. Really, Marcus, I might be beginning to believe in fairy tales but I'm still a practical woman."

"Damn, Skyscraper, she's not falling for your—"

"Shut it, Hollywood! Mind your own damned business." Skyscraper glared at him.

Hollywood chuckled, elbowing Ghost, who sat next to him, then pointing his chin at Skyscraper and Fatima. Ghost grinned, crossing his arms over his chest as he settled back in his seat waiting to see how his buddy would answer the lovely young woman's question.

Growling low, Skyscraper ignored his teammates and turned his attention back to Fatima. "I have contacts that will help me locate your whereabouts. But if it makes you feel better, so you know you can trust in my word, here." He pulled a pen out of his pocket, and reaching for her hand, turned it over. Carefully, he wrote his number on the skin of her inner wrists. "This," he said, kissing the newly-inked digits, "is my private cell number. Don't share it with anyone. Not even those nosy State Department types you're about to meet. Keep your sleeve down," he said, gently unrolling the sleeve of her blue button-down shirt. "When you're finished with them, and you're ready to see me, call me. I'll come running."

Fatima bit her lip, fighting the urge to smile. Her heart was beating wildly, full of happiness. Marcus was serious. He did want to see her again.

"Okay."

"Okay?" he said. "Just, okay, Miss Ali," he teased.

"She said okay, dude." Ghost chuckled. "Stop being so needy."

"Shut up, Allen!" Skyscraper replied, pointing a finger in his direction. "I know where you sleep."

Behind him, Outlaw laughed, then coughed, smothering the sound.

The plane descended, angling in and coming in for a landing. Their idyllic time together was about to end. Still, Fatima was happy. Her Marcus would be only a phone call away.

❧❧❧❧❧ ❧❧❧❧❧

The sun rose over the bayou on what promised to be a hot and humid day. Although it was officially fall, that didn't mean a thing in the south. The hot months ran until winter and even then, the cold was never really very cold. Jersey wiped the sweat from his brow.

"Second hole finished," he said.

Badger reached down clasping Jersey's hand and helped haul him up out of the narrow vertical hole. It was eight feet deep, just like the first one he'd dug ten feet away. Thanks to Google Maps, they found their way deep into the Louisiana backwoods to a quiet bayou far from human traffic. Gators were the real danger here and they had to keep an eye out as they applied shovel to earth a mere twenty feet from a swamp in the dead of night.

When Jersey returned to Mrs. DuBose's house, they went to work immediately rolling up the bodies of the two dead terrorists. The plan was simple. Get the bodies out before Skyscraper's mother came home from the hospital and before the entire neighborhood woke once again. The first Muhammed was long dead, the bullet he'd taken to the head ending his life instantly. The second Muhammed, Daher Tahan, went without a single squeak after Badger sent Jasmin off to bed with the assurance she was safe. In the darkness of the root cellar, Badger moved in behind the unconscious man, lifted his head in his hands, and with one sharp jerk, snapped his neck. Afterwards, he and Jersey commandeered the dead terrorists' rental car, loading the bodies, now rolled in gardening tarps, into the back of the Highlander. it served its purpose well providing enough space in the back for the dead.

With only two hours remaining before dawn, the graves were ready. The men moved to drop each body in, head-first. It was imperative to have the organs at the deepest end of the hole. The blood and fluids would then be so deep that the smell from decomposition would be undetected by curious animals on the surface. The small size of the vertical graves also fooled anyone who might happen upon them. The insignificant mounds would not arouse suspicions.

"Give me the shovel," said Badger.

Jersey handed over the spade they'd filched from Mrs. DuBose's cellar. As the Lieutenant began throwing dirt on top of Muhammed bin Salib's remains, a shrill ring ripped the silence.

Badger froze, looking at Jersey. "Yours?"

Jersey shook his head. "No. One of them."

Badger dropped the shovel. "Shit." He listened. The sound came again, this time a series of beeps indicating a message going to voicemail. It was Bin Salib's phone.

"Dammit. Help me pull him out." Badger and Jersey bent down, grabbing the ankles of the deceased and began to pull. They dragged him free of the hole and cut the rope holding the tarp in place. It was an effort to unravel the dead weight, but they finally got him uncovered.

"Damn, he stinks already," said Jersey, covering his nose.

"Then let's find that phone and get this rotten piece of shit back in the ground. I'd like to get out of here." He reached into the pants pockets rummaging around until he found the cellphone.

"It needs a thumbprint to unlock the screen, Nick," said Badger, fiddling with the phone.

Jersey pulled out his hunting knife and with a swift motion, cut the right-hand thumb from Bin Salib's hand. "Here. You're going to need it more than once."

"Just what I always wanted," he said, casting side-eye at Jersey. "Thanks, dad." Badger made a face and then applied the thumb to the phone's screen.

He flipped through locating the voicemail and listened. When he finished, he threw an anxious look at Jersey.

"Well?"

"We have a problem. The message is from the prince. They failed to check in. A B-team has been activated, and a contract has been ordered on Sulima Ali's head.

Hanging his head, Jersey sighed. "Damn, man. I'm going to need a vacation after this one."

"You and me both, but right now, we need to find the captain. Fatima and her mother are compromised. That goddamned mole has leaked Sulima Ali's whereabouts. Prince Nayef and ISIS have been two steps ahead of us the whole time."

Jersey kicked the dead terrorist. "You miserable fuckers."

Chapter 14

A surprise awaited Skyscraper and the team when they arrived at the Pentagon.

"Doc!" Skyscraper and Outlaw exclaimed in unison as a familiar face joined them in the waiting room outside of General P.K. Davidson's office.

"Did you miss me, fellas?" Jason Lee Gordon, aka, Doc, grinned, reaching out to hug Skyscraper and shake hands with Outlaw.

Hollywood pushed past both and crushed Doc in a bro-hug.

"Shit, man, are you crying?" Doc laughed as Hollywood went quiet.

A muffled reply of "No," sounded suspiciously wobbly. Hollywood sniffed and backed up, slapping Doc on the shoulder.

"Ow!" Doc grabbed his arm and winced.

"What? Shit, man, I'm so sorry," Hollywood began.

"He's fucking with you, Hank," said Ghost, stepping in. "It sure is good to see you, man." He shook Doc's hand who laughed and winked at Hollywood.

"That's not cool, Doc."

"Aw, Hank, I missed you too." Doc patted Hollywood on the back as he moved further into the room. He looked around at his teammates, happy to be back in the fold. "So, what'd I miss?"

Outlaw shook his head and directed the men to take a seat while they waited. "Same shit, different day. Terrorists kidnapping. Terrorists being brought to justice. Good guys save the day."

Doc looked around. "Where's the newbies?"

"Badger and Jersey stayed behind to clean up. They should be here soon. Might not make it before this meeting with the general though."

"And the girl?" Doc asked.

"She's with her mama," Skyscraper answered.

"They let the two of them get together before an SD debriefing? That's unusual."

Outlaw nodded. "Special treatment for desirable assets. With both the mother and the daughter so talented in their field of bio-engineering, and also being in possession of so much knowledge about ISIS—their current plans, locations, and players—the State Department is bending over backwards to make them happy."

"And why not?" asked Skyscraper, throwing a look at his captain. "Neither one is a threat to us. They're both victims and shouldn't be put through any more forced separation bullshit."

Doc's eyebrows shot up. Skyscraper's passionate defense of the ladies Ali was surprising. He was the quiet one, never getting involved in the lives of those they rescued. "Something happen that I should know about?"

Hollywood smirked, a wicked gleam in his eye. "It's just that you're not the only smitten kitten, Doc. You know, the bigger they are, the harder they fall."

Ghost's leg kicked out catching Hollywood in the ankle. Hank jerked and threw a look at Ghost.

"What? Just tellin' the truth."

"Yeah, but sometimes, your timing sucks balls," said Ghost.

Doc's mischievous brown eyes lit up. "Marcus, I had no idea you had a thing for older women."

Skyscraper sat forward, a lethal gleam in his amber eyes. "I'm gonna pretend you didn't say that shit, Doc, on account you've been recuperating, but if you crack wise about Fatima's mother again, I'm gonna kick your ass." He jabbed a finger in Doc's direction punctuating his words.

Smothering a laugh, Doc grew serious. "I'm sorry, man. So young Miss Ali caught your eye, huh? Well, good for you. What's she like?"

"She's smart," said Ghost.

"Brave chick," said Hollywood.

Outlaw rolled his eyes at his men and glanced heavenward before confirming, "She's earned the team's respect, as you can see."

Doc watched Skyscraper whose face relaxed, the murderous glint in his eyes softening.

"She's resourceful. With Baz still in the wind, and with all of us taking point to watch over her she still found ways to protect herself. This girl is fly, Doc. She made homemade flash-bangs and a taser from old cameras and lighters. And my mom and sister really like her. She's sweet too. Caring. Kind. Funny. Doesn't believe in fairytale shit, but at the same time, she's like one of them princesses in an Arabian Night's story, but more badass..." His voice trailed off as the room grew quiet.

The team stared at Skyscraper who suddenly realized he'd said too much.

His eyes narrowed and the murderous glint returned. "Ah, fuck all ya'll!"

The men burst out laughing and Doc leaned forward patting Skyscraper's shoulder. As they enjoyed their reunion and the familiar razzing, the door to the general's office opened and the man himself stepped out.

"Stop all that schoolgirl giggling and get in here. We've got a problem."

❧❧❧❧❧ ❧❧❧❧❧

Fatima hugged her mother. Sulima Ali stroked her daughter's hair and whispered soothing sounds. Earlier, an Intelligence officer named Natalie Greenblatt came to take their statements. She'd been accompanied by a gentleman named Adam Jones, an aide to the Secretary of State. He was not a pleasant person, but Ms. Greenblatt made up for that with her professionalism. For every question she asked, he butted in asking counter-questions like *"And did you have relations with these ISIS fighters prior to your alleged kidnapping, Miss Ali?"*

His inference was insulting, and he seemed determined to paint a picture of collusion between the Ali women and the kidnappers. Even Ms. Greenblatt was annoyed if the side-eye she threw at Jones was any indication.

"What Mr. Jones means is," she gave Jones a pointed look before addressing Sulima Ali, *"did you ever come across Omar Baz or any of the men working with him prior to the attack on your family and death of your husband?"*

Sulima glared at Jones before turning her attention to Greenblatt. "I did not. Neither did my daughter. We came from the UAE, from Dubai to Syria only on a wellness check for Tariq's family. He had not been back to Syria for three years, and with the civil war outbreak, he was concerned for them. We all were."

The rest of the interview passed with the women in the room ignoring Adam Jones as much as was possible.

"That man is odious!" Fatima declared when they'd been released back to their hotel.

"Yes, he is. I wonder what he thought to gain from behaving like such an ass?" Sulima stared out the window of their room in the Ritz-Carlton near the Pentagon. The room was provided courtesy of the State Department until they decided what, exactly to do with them. The suite was quite comfortable. It had a separate living room from the bedroom with views of Arlington. The subtle grays and sharp whites mixed with dark contemporary wood created a calm atmosphere. There was a king-size bed in the single bedroom and the living room sofa pulled out into a full-size bed. The bathroom had marble walls and vanity. Truly luxurious after what they'd both gone through. They were even allowed access to the club dining, but for now, ordering in room service seemed easier than trying to summon the energy to deal with people.

Fatima ordered for them both when they arrived in their room; two cups of onion soup with Gruyere and croutons and organic chicken breasts with broccolini, carrots, and peas with an almond verjus. It sounded wonderful, but once the food arrived, neither had the appetite to do it justice.

Now, they huddled together on the sofa trying to figure out what came next.

"He was trying to find a reason to deny our asylum," she said, still fuming over the odious troll, Adam Jones.

Sulima frowned. "We have too much to offer. They won't deny the request, but he did seem determined to find fault." She pulled back and looked down at Fatima. She smiled, tucking a strand of her daughter's hair behind her ear. "I'm so grateful right now. I don't want that man ruining the best day of my life. I have my Fatima back." She sniffed, her eyes tearing up.

"Don't cry, mother. We made it." Fatima gently wiped the tears away. "Somehow, we got through it and now we're safe, together again."

"Thanks be to God," she said, hugging Fatima tightly once again. "I don't know what I would've done if anything happened to you. I must thank the nice soldiers. Will we be seeing them again?"

Fatima smiled into her mother's shoulder. "Yes, I believe we will be seeing Marcus again."

"Marcus, is it? Which one is he again?" her mother chuckled.

"The handsome one," she replied wistfully. "The one they call Skyscraper."

"Ah, the tall one. Yes, he is quite handsome." Sulima looked down into her daughter's face. "He behaved respectfully with you?"

Thoughts of their kiss flashed through her memory, his hands caressing her backside, his hardness pressing into her. She fought the blush threatening to bloom in her cheeks. "Yes, mother. Marcus kept me safe, and he was always a gentleman. They all were."

"Good. I'd hate to have to take him to task after rescuing us both." She noted the glow in her daughter's face. "I take it you like Marcus?"

Fatima sat up, pulling her knees to her chest before wrapping her arms around them. "He is kind, mother. And brave, and considerate. You know, he plays piano, like his father before him."

"Oh, he does, does he? Sounds like you got to know him rather well."

"His mother and sister are also very nice. They live in New Orleans. That's where we were before coming here."

"You've had quite an adventure, my love, but try not to expect too much. What was an adventure for you was just another mission for your Marcus. This is what he does. It's romantic to you, but for him, it is work."

Her mother's words hit a nerve. "I'm not one to day-dream about fairytales, mother. You know this. And Marcus is an honorable man. He promised I would see him again and I believe him."

Sulima heard the certainty in Fatima's words, saw the absolute trust in her eyes. It was true, even as a child, Fatima would rather read science books than have children's stories read to her. She did not spend her time with her head in the clouds, and yet, here she was, practically gushing and sounding for all the world like a young woman smitten.

"Well, for your sake, I do hope Marcus is everything you've described. Otherwise, I will have to have words with him. If he comes around, I may still do so. Since your father is not here to determine this young man's intentions, it falls to me."

"Oh, mother!" Fatima laughed.

"I'm serious," Sulima replied, but there was a twinkle in her eyes.

"Don't embarrass me."

"I make no such promise."

"Mother!"

Sulima grinned, happiness filling her heart. To be able to have this time with her daughter was a miracle. For over a year, she feared she'd never see her again or that if she did, Fatima would be damaged beyond repair. Somehow, by God's grace, they'd both survived, and her daughter had not been ruined. To see her experiencing this crush or whatever it was, was a gift. Fatima managed to pick up the pieces and keep herself together. Perhaps Marcus was the reason. If so, she would be forever grateful.

Chapter 15

Fatima awoke with joy in her heart. Her mother's light snore next to her all night was the most welcome sound she could think of, and she smiled. The night before, her mother offered her the bed insisting she would sleep on the pull-out, but Fatima was having none of it. Pointing out that the single bed was king-sized, she decided for them both to share it.

"There's plenty of room mother, and I don't want to be so far away from you. Please." Sulima could not refuse.

As normal as Fatima seemed, there was still a bit of the lost little girl in her daughter. She couldn't deny the logic or the subtle persuasion of her words. It was obvious Fatima needed her close. Sulima needed that closeness too. Together, they curled up in the middle of the big bed and for the first time in over a year, slept peacefully.

In the early hours of dawn, Fatima listened to the sound of her mother singing in the shower. There was only one other thing that could make her happier than she felt now. She reached for the phone on the nightstand, and glancing at the ink still staining her wrist, dialed the number. It went straight to voicemail.

She hung up, not wanting to disturb Marcus should he be working. She suspected he was. As a soldier, did he ever have any down time? She didn't know the answer. Her mother came out of the bathroom, a towel wrapped around her wet hair.

"Rise and shine, daughter. The day awaits. We can enjoy breakfast together and then Ms. Greenblatt wants to meet with us. She's sending a car at 8:30, so get your lazy bones into the shower.

Fatima dropped her feet to the floor, sitting on the edge of the comfortable mattress. "Did she say what it's about?"

"No, but it's surely to do with our application for asylum." Sulima approached her daughter, sitting next to her and taking her hand. "We must prepare ourselves for the possibility it will be denied."

"What? Why?"

"There are no guarantees for immigrants here in the U.S., Fatima. Especially right now. We're lucky to be here," she looked around the posh hotel room, sighing, "rather than in a detention center." She patted her daughter's hand. "Go, get cleaned up. We must always present our very best selves."

Fatima's brow creased as she pondered her mother's words. She knew better than most that anything could happen and much of it not good. Still, America was the shining beacon on the hill. It was the great American melting pot, a place for those looking to start life anew and live the dream. The words engraved on the Statue of Liberty at Ellis Island were known around the globe, even in the darkest corners.

Give me your tired, your poor, your huddled masses yearning to breathe free, The wretched refuse of your teeming shore. Send these, the homeless, tempest-tossed to me, I lift my lamp beside the golden door!

She stood under the hot spray lathering her hair, her thoughts running ninety miles a minute. '*We can't go back. If we step one toe back into Dubai, anywhere in the UAE, we'll be taken again or killed. We've done this right according to their laws. Why would they send us away? We have so much to offer! And what about Marcus...*'

Fatima's ire rose with each question, but the last one broke her heart. If the U.S. denied their request, if they sent her and her mother back, she'd likely never see Marcus again. He meant so much to her, but until that moment, she hadn't realized exactly how much.

In the next room, Sulima stood in front of the dresser mirror brushing the tangles from her long hair. Carefully, she divided it into two sections and began braiding each. As she wove the strands, a red light blinked reflected in the glass. She looked to the corner of the mirror seeing nothing. Again, it blinked. It was coming from the vent over the bed behind her. She turned, tying off the second braid and stared at the wall. The vent cover was slightly askew with one screw missing. She approached, climbing up onto the bed in order to reach the area. As she raised her hand, a knock sounded at the door.

Backing up, she climbed down, and quickly threw on a shirt and pants before leaving the bedroom.

A concierge stood in the hallway, a bouquet of flowers in his hands.

"Good morning, ma'am. These arrived at the desk. There's no name on the card. Only the room number. I didn't wish to pry." He handed over the dozen red roses.

"How lovely," she said. "Thank you. Oh, wait, I should tip you," she said, looking around for the small clutch she'd been given recently after arriving.

The concierge backed up, his hands at his sides. "No need, madame. Everything for this room is already covered, tips included. Have a nice day and don't hesitate to call if there's anything you need."

"I will, thank you again." Sulima closed the door, throwing the lock automatically. She looked around and found an open space on the coffee table. Setting the vase of roses down, she looked for the card. There was one stuck into a floral pick just as the concierge said. Only the room number adorned the outside of the small envelope. It was sealed. She couldn't think who might be sending her roses but after the discussion with Fatima the night before, she had a sneaking suspicion they were for her. Smiling, she replaced the card and waited for her daughter to finish her ablutions. Perhaps the tall soldier did have feelings for Fatima and there was no reason to worry over his intentions. Roses were always a good sign. Red roses were even better because red was the color of love.

Leaving the pretty bouquet on the table, she went back to finish getting ready for breakfast. There was new hope in her old heart. The floral delivery felt like a good omen for the rest of their day. As she returned to the room, she hummed a happy tune, the red blinking light in the vent above the bed already forgotten.

⟫⟫⟫ ⟪⟪⟪

Skyscraper rubbed the grit from his tired eyes. He'd barely slept four hours. The only good news came from the quick call he'd put in to his sister. Mr. Emmet was going to be okay. The bullet hit his right shoulder shattering the man's fragile bones. He'd undergone surgery to replace part of the joint and would need a lot of therapy afterwards, but he was a tough old codger. He'd even made sure to send along a message to Marcus. *"Tell him don't worry 'bout me. Jesus has my back. Tell him just go handle his business, and I'm proud of him."* That made him smile, but the meeting with the general had not gone well. A relay of contacts conveyed a message from Badger and Jersey. There was another team of terrorists unaccounted for. According to the message found on the deceased Muhammed bin Salib's burner phone, since the prince had not heard back from Baz or the Muhammeds, a follow-up team had been activated. This one's orders were to eliminate the A-team and then locate and terminate Sulima Ali. That was bad enough, but the worst part was the last line.

"Our contact is already tracking you and the women. Remember, there's no escape!"

The mole within COM-SAD had been busy and they still didn't know who it was. At this point, they weren't even sure if the mole was inside COM-SAD or higher up.

The general put a call in to Rio Taggart who said he had only just discovered a lead.

"Well get the hell on it, Rio! This somabitch is threatening our own and I am not having it." the general bellowed.

"Sir, yessir. I'm on it. It would help if I had the phone with the message. I could trace the source then."

"We'll get it to you as soon as possible but in the meantime, you follow up on whatever lead you've uncovered. We haven't got much time." A vein throbbed in General Davidson's temple as he pounded the table with his fist. "Goddammit.

Skyscraper interrupted. "What about the number of the phone, Rio?" he asked, looking down at the intercom speaker. "You know, the I.D. number inside? Would that help?"

"As a matter of fact, Sky, it would. You got it?" Rio asked.

Outlaw shook his head. "No, we don't, but you can get it from Badger. That'll be faster than waiting on the government to deliver it. You got his number?"

"I do. What I don't understand is why he didn't call me first? Why the five-part relay through Black Site Alpha?"

"That's my fault, Rio. I didn't give Badger your number. Pretty sure right now he doesn't have mine either or else he would've called me directly. We haven't been out of two-way range until now."

"I see. That does explain it. Okay, I'm putting in the call now. Should have a trace within the next several hours."

"Good," said General Davidson. He disconnected the call and faced Outlaw. "That was a first-class fuck-up, Nate. Any delay in communications can cost lives. You know this."

Outlaw stiffened but took his lumps like a man. "I take full responsibility, General. It won't happen again."

"It goddamned better not! Everyone," he said, looking around the room, "get to quarters and grab a few hours of rest. It won't be much, but I need you all fully alert. Until this threat is neutralized, you're all on my shit list. Dismissed!"

Skyscraper's ears were still ringing from the reaming. The general was right though. They all deserved that dressing down. Fatima and her mother were still in danger. Worse, he didn't know where the State Department had put them up. He hoped it was at quarters within the Pentagon. It was the only safe place right now. He'd tried to ask the general's secretary but all she could confirm was that the ladies were settled and had a surveillance team in place for their safety.

He got up and headed for the dormitory showers down the hall. After washing up, he felt revived. The team was meeting for breakfast and there were plans to make, all of them dependent upon what Rio found. He hoped there were coordinates pinning down a location because he was ready to put an end to all of this. Once Fatima was free from anymore threats to her life, he wanted to ask her out on a date. A real one, with flowers, candlelight, and dinner at a nice restaurant. He wanted to take her dancing under the stars. The idea of holding her in his arms again brought a smile to his face. Like his mama always said, hold onto the hope.

Fatima was his hope.

Chapter 16

Fatima could not prevent the smile on her face if her life depended on it. She held the tiny card in her hands reading it again.

"Meet me at the Lincoln Memorial at noon for lunch."

Sulima ate her eggs, trying not to laugh at the radiant expression in her daughter's eyes.

"Are you going to tell me what Mr. Wonderful said or not?"

Fatima put the card inside the pocket of her red blouse. It was borrowed from her mother who had several new outfits provided for her courtesy of the government. She felt that was a good sign. If they were planning on sending them back to Dubai, she was sure they wouldn't bother with providing a wardrobe. The black slacks and low-heeled shoes made her feel more like her old self. It was a good thing she and her mother wore the same size.

"Nope. It's private," she hedged, grinning. "But I think he misses me," she said, peeling and popping a slice of orange into her mouth. She didn't want to share the details of her rendezvous yet. Absolutely, she would tell her mother later, after they found out what the State Department planned for them. If she couldn't make it to the Lincoln Memorial for any reason, she could call him. Until then, she just wanted to be a young woman anticipating a lunch date with a handsome man.

"Okay, missy. I'll let you keep your secrets for now, but I expect you to tell me something later. Anything. I'm dying to know!" Sulima chuckled. "It's not every day my little girl is in love."

"Mother! I'm not in love," she said. "I just really like him. A lot."

"Um hmm. I know. I remember that exact look the first time your father asked me on a date."

At the mention of her father, some of Fatima's happiness faded. She missed him terribly. She could not fathom how hard it had been for her mother to lose her husband. Now that she'd met Marcus, she could imagine what that pain was like. If something happened to him, her heart would break. Was that love? She didn't know, but it was clear that as good as love could make one feel, it cut both ways.

"Do you miss papa?"

Sulima put down her cutlery. Placing her hands in her lap, she looked out the window of the clubhouse restaurant inside the hotel. "I spent the last year trying so hard not to think about what we've lost, but now, since coming to America, I've had nothing but time. It's hard most days just to get out of bed in the morning. I keep rolling over and reaching for Tariq, but he's not there." She looked at her daughter. "I miss him so much, it hurts. Deep down in my bones there is pain. But I look at you, Fatima, and I'm so grateful. I see his intelligence and his kind heart in you. Tariq is not truly gone from us. He lives on forever in our hearts and in our memories. Together, we will honor him by living the best life possible." She reached out, taking Fatima's hands. "And that begins with today. First, our meeting with the State Department, and then, my beautiful girl, you will tell me more about your Marcus."

Fatima sniffed, her eyes stinging with unshed tears. "Everything is going to be alright, mother. I feel it."

"Good. Then let's get our new life started. If you're finished, we can go, yes?"

With a nod, Fatima tossed her napkin onto the table, downed the last of her orange juice, and pushed back her chair. "Yes. Let's begin."

Together, the two Ali women made their way down-stairs to a waiting car. The rest of the morning was a whirlwind of short meetings. Their request for asylum was accepted, but with conditions. Part of those condi-tions required Sulima to come work for the Department of Defense bio-engineering division. Another condition had Fatima being enrolled in online advanced bio-engi-neering courses as well as starting an internship with the leading business in that field. WinRunner. Oddly, and luckily enough, they would both be sent to the same fa-cility. Camp Lazarus, Nevada. That, however, was where Fatima's luck ran out.

Natalie Greenblatt's words were stern. "Under no cir-cumstance can you tell anyone where you'll be going. This is a top-secret facility. Violation of this confidential-ity agreement will result in immediate revocation of your asylum status. No ifs, ands, or buts. Understood?

Sulima nodded her agreement while Fatima hesitated. "Ms. Greenblatt, there is someone..."

"No one," she reiterated. And then, giving a pointed stare, added, "Not even Sergeant DuBose. Yes, we've been made aware of how close you've become. That's under-standable under the circumstances. However, not even the sergeant can know of this facility. You'll be allowed to make calls out once a week and you can write letters, but both the calls and the address for the letters will conceal your true location."

Greenblatt's words stung. Fatima did not want to be apart from Marcus. Indeed, she didn't know how a relationship would even be possible given the restrictions and distance. She didn't even know if she'd be allowed to leave the facility. Her afternoon lunch date might just be their last. She knew without a doubt now that she would not miss it.

Sulima saw the distress in her daughter's eyes. Turning to Natalie Greenblatt, she blurted, "What about spouses?"

Greenblatt blinked. "Spouses have to sign NDRs. They would be bound by the same confidentiality as you, but that's not the case here," she said, looking at Fatima. "Is it?

She shook her head. "No." But it was enough to lift Fatima's spirits. Hope sprang eternal.

"There's going to be a lot of paperwork and then I'd like to sit you both down with Joely Winter in the next room. She's the head of WinRunner and a biotech prodigy. We were lucky to get her to sign on with the DOD."

The rest of the morning was busy, and time passed quickly. Before long it was time for lunch. Fatima asked to be excused, and then, taking one last look behind her at the conference room, slipped out into the hall and out the front door. Within moments, she hailed a taxi.

"The Lincoln Memorial, please."

The driver nodded and merged into traffic moving with increasing speed away from the Pentagon.

꧁꧂ ꧁꧂

"I've ID'd the burner phone and traced the incoming calls to that number. There were three and they took a damned long time to trace. Lots of relays pinging across the globe," said Rio.

"And? Don't leave us in suspense, Taggart!" The general barked, already pissed off in anticipation of Rio's news.

Outlaw and his team sat around the desk staring at the computer screen. Rio's face was solemn as he viewed the team members he could see on the DOD face-time video chat.

"The first was from a number inside King's Palace in Riyadh."

"Them sons-of-bitches," muttered General Davidson. "Has to be Nayef. He keeps apartments there with his big brother, the crown prince."

Outlaw nodded and looked at Rio. "Who else, Rio?"

"The second was from another burner phone purchased in Jacksonville, Florida. Had to be the B-team. I'm guessing a sleeper cell. That same phone pinged once in Alabama and again in Louisiana. They drove there. I don't have a line on who they are yet. Still running down exactly where and when the phone was purchased. The last number, though, is the most revealing. General, you're going to need to take immediate action."

The general drummed his fingers, the vein quietly throbbing in his temple. "Just spill it, son, so we can move."

Outlaw and his team leaned in, everyone holding their breath. Skyscraper focused like a laser, a bad feeling churning in his gut.

"The last number came from inside the State Department. Two calls. One two days ago." Rio glanced at Outlaw. "Around the time your team arrived in New Orleans. The second time clocked in right after you called me to send in the cavalry and move you all out to Arlington."

Outlaw and Skyscraper exchanged a look.

"I thought only Rio had your number," said Skyscraper.

Outlaw looked at Rio. "There's only one other official kept apprised of our activities."

Rio nodded. "That's right. The Secretary of State."

The general's eyes narrowed as he held his breath. "Whose line did the call come from, Taggart?"

Rio threw a screenshot of the number up onto the monitor. "Adam Jones, sir."

A fist pounded the desk and Outlaw cursed.

General Davidson exploded. "That twitchy little brown-noser? Shit!" The general pulled out his cell phone and hit a number on speed dial. "Get me the Director." He waited as he was patched through to the FBI. "Thomas," he said, "we have a traitor in our midst. I need your team to locate Secretary Morgan's aide Adam Jones and arrest him. Needs to be quick. We have evidence he's the mole leaking intelligence on our Spec Ops team. And find out who inside of COM-SAD he's been using. He's not doing this alone. He's got some peckerwood helping him. Yeah. I'll have Taggart send over the evidence, but you've got to move now. My boys' lives are at stake, and we have a sleeper cell of fucking terrorists still in the wind. On goddamned U.S. soil, no less! Get back with me as soon as you have Jones. Also, we need to meet with the president ASAP. We have a Saudi situation."

No sooner had the general hung up before a head poked through the conference room door. A young private, looking rattled, spoke. "Sir, I'm sorry to interrupt, but—"

"What is it, Jacobs?" the general barked.

"Natalie Greenblatt is on the line, says it's urgent. Something about a missing girl. A Fatima somebody or other..."

Skyscraper jumped up. "What happened?"

The general stood, holding up a hand at Skyscraper. "Cool your jets, Sergeant." He looked at Jacobs. "Patch her through on line two."

"Yes, sir." Jacobs left and a few seconds later, line two rang.

The general answered the call on speaker phone. "Natalie, what in God's name is going on?"

"General, we might have a problem. I'm not sure yet though."

"What is it?"

"Fatima Ali has gone missing. She was here but left after we finished up paperwork on our end. We've confirmed she never returned to the hotel room. Her mother did mention a note Fatima received with a bouquet of roses this morning. She thinks maybe Fatima went off to meet Sergeant DuBose."

The general looked at Skyscraper. The panic in DuBose's face told him all he needed to know. "Dubose is here with me now. By the fear in his eyes, I feel safe in saying he knew nothing about this."

"No sir. I did not send any flowers," said Skyscraper. "Something's wrong."

Outlaw placed a restraining hand on Skyscraper's shoulder. He could feel the man's need to run out the door, but they needed more information.

"Does her mother have any idea where she went?" Outlaw asked.

Greenblatt answered. "None, but we pulled up surveillance of the building. CCTV shows her getting into a local cab. We're tracking down the driver now. He should have an address."

"When will you know?" Skyscraper asked, pain in his voice.

"Anytime now. We've contacted the taxi company's main dispatch. They're tracking down the driver. Should be soon."

"Put a rush on it! Fatima would never go anywhere unless I told her to do so. If someone is imitating me somehow, she's unprotected!"

"Hold on," said Greenblatt. The sound of a phone ringing interrupted them. She answered. "Yeah. And when was this? Is he sure it was her? Red shirt, black slacks? Okay. Where did he take her?"

Skyscraper felt his blood pressure rising. He was ready to kill. He knew he would if anything had happened to Fatima.

Greenblatt came back on the line. "He took her to the Lincoln Memorial, picked her up forty minutes ago. The driver said he dropped her there about ten minutes ago.

Said she was in good spirits and didn't seem to be in distress. I have a feeling she was lured out."

The general thanked Natalie. Looking at Outlaw and Skyscraper, and then glancing at Ghost, Hollywood, Doc, and Badger and Jersey, who'd joined them an hour earlier, he gave the order. "Get over there. Find the girl."

Skyscraper asked the pressing question. "And if we encounter the B-team?"

The general didn't flinch. "Take them out. We'll spin any fallout later."

Outlaw coordinated quickly with transportation. The fastest way there at this hour was by helicopter. The general approved the order for a VH-60 Black Hawk. ETA was five minutes to lift off. That was just enough time to hit up the weapons locker.

As they climbed into the helo, strapping on their helmets, Skyscraper was losing his mind. All he could think of was he'd failed her—again. He'd trusted in the State Department to protect her, and he'd been wrong. He didn't know who he could trust anymore. One thing was certain, when he found her this time, he would not let her go.

Ghost and Outlaw noted the look of fear in Skyscraper's amber eyes. Never had they seen him this way. The man was always cool, calm, and deadly. The difference now was he was not calm, he was panicked. This was bad news for the terrorists. The violence he reserved for the bad guys was amplified a thousand-fold. Outlaw remembered that feeling. He'd gone through it with Emma.

Next to Skyscraper, Doc worried aloud for his friend. "It's going to be alright, man. We'll find her. And we'll put an end to these ISIS motherfuckers."

Skyscraper looked at Doc. He held out his fist. Doc bumped it with his own. "Hoorah, Doc. Let's go kill some bad guys." Glancing at Outlaw and Hollywood, he added, "And don't try and stop me."

"I wouldn't dream of it, buddy. I got your back," said Hollywood.

"You've got the Com on this one, Skyscraper," said Outlaw. "We're following you."

The Black Hawk lifted off, moving fast towards the west end of the National Mall and to the Lincoln Memorial. It was five minutes past noon on a Tuesday.

Chapter 17

F atima walked the length of the mall moving toward the famous Lincoln Memorial. She'd read about it and all the other points of interest in D.C., but this would be the first time she would see it with her own eyes. Joy filled her heart because she knew she would be seeing it with Marcus. As she drew closer, she looked around, trying to find her tall, handsome soldier. He would be easy to find in the crowd, being at least a head and shoulders taller than most.

People came and went, some with baby strollers, others in school groups. Even in fall on a Tuesday afternoon, it was busy. Excitement grew when she arrived at the main steps. Looking up, she saw the massive statue of Abraham Lincoln sitting in his chair. Above his head it read, "*In this temple, as in the hearts of the people for whom he saved the Union, the memory of Abraham Lincoln is enshrined forever.*"

It was a somber moment for Fatima. This was the 16th president of the United States, a country she would call home after her time cooperating with the government and the Department of Defense. She wanted to learn more, but her curiosity was only exceeded by her excitement to see Marcus. She turned, looking through the crowd. Surely, he would find her here. She glanced down at the watch on her wrist, a cheap gold-toned Timex borrowed from her mother. It was five minutes past noon. Marcus was late.

She walked back toward the stairs. A bearded man bumped into her.

"Sorry," he said. "You have the time?" He tapped his bare wrist.

Fatima looked at him. He was around six feet tall with swarthy skin. His beard was trimmed close to his face, neatly manicured and his glossy black hair cut short. He wore a nondescript Navy blue, long-sleeved sweatshirt and dark blue casual slacks.

"Sure. It's six minutes past noon," she answered.

"Many thanks," he said.

Fatima turned to leave. His hand grabbed her upper arm, squeezing painfully.

"Scream and I'll kill you on the spot. Come. Move." He jerked her arm, directing her down the steps.

Panic seized her. "Who are you?"

"Shup up! No talking. If you try to get anyone to help you, I'll kill them too."

Something solid poked into her back. Fatima knew it was the barrel of a gun pressed into her left kidney. He was serious.

Down the steps they went. Fear coursed through her body making her limbs feel leaden. She tried not to trip over her own feet. Pieces of the puzzle fell into place in her mind. "You sent me the flowers?"

He laughed. "Of course. And you fell for it. Stupid woman. Doesn't matter though. The prince has ordered your death."

Fatima mentally berated herself. She'd thought, without proof or even a signature, that Marcus had sent her flowers, had invited her out. Her own foolishness had brought her to this danger. No one knew where she was. Marcus would not save her this time. He didn't even know she was missing. Panic filled her and tears welled in her eyes. She blinked them away. She had to think!

If this man succeeded in steering her out of the crowd, she was as good as dead. She had to break away from him. Here. Now.

Lifting her foot, she brought the heel down on his toes. The man yelped in pain, his grip loosening. Twisting, Fatima pulled free and began to run. Ahead, two more men standing near a parked van came running at her. The man behind her shouted, "Get her!"

Fatima broke right dodging between tourists, three terrorists hot on her trail. The wind kicked up flattening the grass around her as she ran. The sound of blades whipping through the air grew louder, but she could not stop and look to see what was happening. If she slowed down for even a second, they'd have her. She drew air into her lungs and forced her legs to move faster.

The sound of raised voices grew to shouts of alarm. People began running in all directions away from the National Mall. A loud rata-tat-tat of machine gun fire ripped through the cacophony of screams. Fatima felt her heart jump in her chest, her lungs burning as she reached a parking lot on the other side of the mall. There, she dove behind a parked green pickup truck for cover.

※※※ ※※※

Skyscraper jumped out of the Black Hawk before it fully landed, breaking into a sprint immediately. They'd spotted Fatima thanks to the description of her clothing. Three men chased her across the lawn of the National Mall. Skyscraper took the lead, moving fast and closing the distance between himself and the three men chasing his woman.

Something primal bubbled up inside him. He saw red. None of those men would see tomorrow.

Behind him, Outlaw, Ghost, and Hollywood broke left while Badger and Jersey went right. They created a net formation as they closed in on the B-team terrorists. Thankfully, the civilians had cleared out the moment they saw the Black Hawk and heard the machine gun fire. A few stragglers stood off to the side like idiots filming the unfolding scene on their cell phones, oblivious to the danger they were in.

The first of the three terrorists was now a mere four feet from Skyscraper's reach. He lunged, grabbing the man by the neck of his shirt. He yanked him backwards, drew his hunting blade from its sheath, and in a quick rolling motion, cut the man's throat. When they came to a stop, the terrorist was already dead. Skyscraper didn't spare him a second glance. He took off again, going for the remaining two. The closest one turned, and seeing they had company, shouted a warning to his leader.

Badger and Jersey moved in from the right. The man, shorter than his leader and stockier, tried going left. Outlaw and Ghost had him dead to rights. Ghost took aim, pulling the trigger, and sent a spray of bullets flying.

Jerking with each hit, the stocky terrorist went down, gun still in hand.

The last one, thinking the team distracted, put on an extraordinary burst of speed heading for the parking lot and the green truck Fatima had run behind for cover.

Skyscraper hurdled over the dead body on the ground hot on his tail.

The B-team leader reached the green pickup truck. "Come out, Fatima Ali. It's over!"

"You're goddamned right about that, motherfucker. It's over all right, for you!" Skyscraper dove, his arm coming around the man's neck.

The man countered, shoving his hand in between like a wedge while throwing an elbow. Skyscraper took the jab and squeezed tighter, refusing to let go. He heard bones crunch. The man's fingers broke, caught between his jaw and Skyscraper's arm. Like a boa constrictor, he methodically cut off the man's air. His face bloomed bright red and his elbow jabs grew weaker. He sputtered but could not draw breath. Slowly, his limbs went lax. The red of his face turned blue and with the last of his life sputtering, his bladder drained with it. The scent of urine filled the air.

Skyscraper held on even after he was sure the man was dead. The fury within still controlled him. To his horror, Fatima stepped out from behind the truck.

"Get her out of here, Hollywood," he yelled, his eyes welling, his words tortured. "Get her out!"

Hollywood moved to stand between Fatima and the death scene in front of the truck. She pushed Hollywood away.

"No," she said, moving around him.

She made her way to Skyscraper who backed up, still gripping the dead man.

"Don't look at me, Fatima. Please!" His voice broke. The expression on her face tore at his heart. Shock, horror. He'd caused that. He couldn't bear for her to see him like this, to see him in kill mode. It was his worst fear.

"Marcus, please. It's okay. Come to me," she whispered, tears sliding down her cheeks. She opened her arms.

Outlaw approached him from the side cautiously. "Marcus, let go. Here," he said, reaching to remove the dead man from his grip. "I've got him. Let go."

Skyscraper released the dead weight but hesitated. "I can't, Fatima. I can't. Please look away, please." He shook his head repeatedly, backing up. He couldn't go to her, couldn't hold her, not with arms that had just killed. She was too good for that, too good for him. And yet, she stood there still, entreating him to come to her, arms wide open. His eyes widened, shocked.

"Marcus, my sweet Marcus. It's okay. I'm okay. I'm safe thanks to you. You saved me."

"But it's my fault you were in danger to begin with."

"No, it wasn't. It was my own foolishness this time." She pulled the card out of her shirt pocket holding it up. "See?" she said, tears blurring her vision. "I thought you'd invited me out on a date. I was so stupid. So you see, it wasn't your fault."

Her tears broke him completely. "That's not stupid. I want to. I planned to. I was going to ask you out," he said. His emotions burst the damn and he rushed to her. Forgetting everything, he pulled her into his arms. "Fatima, I've thought of nothing else. Believe me, baby. I'm so sorry. So sorry..." he said, his voice raw, "but you have to remember never go anywhere—"

"Unless you come to my door. Unless it's you," she sniffed. "Oh, Marcus, I'm so sorry." She buried her face in his chest, sobbing. "I should have known better."

He kissed the top of her head. "It wasn't your fault. You couldn't have known, but for future reference, I will always deliver flowers in person, just so you know they're from me."

She glanced up. "In future? We have a future?"

He sucked in a breath, hoping against hope. "Yes, ma'am, we do. At least," he said, gently pushing the hair from her eyes and tucking the strands behind her ear, "I hope we do." They stared at each other, lost in the moment, and forgetting the world around them.

"I want nothing more than to take you on a real date, Miss Ali."

She inhaled a wobbly breath. "Dinner and dancing?"

"Anything you want, beautiful. Is that a yes?"

Fatima bit her lip. "Yes. It is. A yes, that is."

"And you don't mind dating a man that..." his voice trailed off as his eyes looked sideways at the dead man now lying at Outlaw's feet.

"A man who protects me? A man who would kill to keep me safe? No, I don't mind. Marcus, you're not a bad man." She gripped his Kevlar vest. "You are a good man who stops the bad ones. Don't you know that yet?" She reached up placing her warm palm against his cheek. "I knew it right away. It's why I lo—"

He swooped down, his lips locking on hers in a deep, passionate kiss. There, in a parking lot on the National Mall, surrounded now by the military and local police, and with three dead terrorists littering the grounds, the world melted away. It was only the two of them, and nothing else mattered.

Ghost cleared his throat. "Uh, buddy. You're being filmed by a bunch of civilian yahoos. You might want to cool your jets until we get to a more secure location."

Skyscraper pulled back and glanced around. Keeping Fatima close he whispered, "Let's get out of here."

"Yes, please." She let him lead the way back to the waiting Black Hawk. After helping her aboard and strapping her seatbelt around her he whispered, "And me, too."

"What?" she asked.

He dropped a quick kiss on her lips. "I love you too, Miss Ali."

"Oh!" she blushed.

Skyscraper took her hand, holding it as the helo lifted off. The heaviness in his heart faded as he contemplated just how lucky he was to have found the one woman in the world who could understand the life of a soldier. One who could look past the trained killer to the man beneath. For the first time in his life, he felt truly hopeful, and that hope bubbled over into a goofy smile.

"What is it?" she asked. "What are you thinking about, Marcus?"

The grin grew. "You, beautiful. I'm thinking about you. And our date."

"Oh, yes? What are you planning?"

He thought for a moment. "Something you said you'd like to do. No spoilers. It's going to be a surprise. Just you wait."

"A surprise? Marcus, tell me?" She pulled at his hand.

"Nope. You're gonna have to wait, but I promise, you'll like it. Or, at least, I hope you will."

She noticed a shyness in his amber eyes, an adorable boyishness so unlike the confident soldier she knew. It was unusual for Marcus to exhibit any insecurity, but it was mixed with so much hope that she couldn't help but laugh. "I know I will. Oh, Marcus, I'm so excited. I can't believe this is all happening, and I have so much to tell you."

"Save it for our date, okay? Let's just...be. Let's just soak in this moment together. You're finally free. We're safe now."

"No more crazy?"

"No, baby, no more crazy."

"Okay. Good. Then, hold me." She snuggled closer.

Skyscraper put his arm around her. Having her settled against him just felt right. Like it was always meant to be. He looked around the interior of the helicopter. Outlaw sat back, arms crossed over his chest, grinning. Hollywood gave him a thumbs up. Ghost silently applauded the couple. Badger and Jersey smothered their smiles while sharing a fist-bump. Only Doc spoke.

"So, double wedding? Me and Leisl and you and Fatima?"

Skyscraper bit back the snarky reply always ready on the tip of his tongue. He was too happy to rise to the bait. Instead, he grinned, and replied, "Maybe."

Chapter 18

Fatima stared into Marcus's eyes. He looked so hand-some tonight, she thought. Her tall, brave, wonder-ful soldier wore a black suit with a starched white shirt beneath. He sported a fresh haircut and even had a dashing royal blue silk handkerchief neatly folded and displayed in his jacket pocket. The cuffs of his shirt were fastened with an antique pair of gold cuff links decorated in musical notes created with diamond chips. They belonged to his father and his father's father before him. Fitting the for-mality of the evening, she wore a shimmering ankle-length gown in mermaid colors of sea green, blue, and deep pur-ple. Silver heels complimented by silver jewelry completed the ensemble—all gifts from her Marcus. She wore her long black hair swept up atop her head allowing a few curls to hang down. Skyscraper took her to a five-star restau-rant for dinner, and afterwards, to a small club. There, he surprised her by joining the jazz quartet on stage. It was, indeed, a pleasant surprise and she loved it.

She watched as he sat behind the piano playing a sultry number. She sipped white wine as the music flowed. He was impressive. There was clearly the soul of a musician living beneath the surface of the soldier. How he ended up in the military and not on stage somewhere she didn't know, but she was thankful. He'd saved her life, not once, not twice, but three times.

Now, they were enjoying their date, and he was serenading her with song. It was almost like a fairytale.

Every keystroke struck a chord within vibrating throughout her body. As she watched his large hands skim over the ivories, she imagined his fingers finding all the right keys on her. Heat suffused her cheeks. Whether it was the wine or her illicit thoughts, she didn't care. Tonight was about celebrating her new life, her freedom, and just being a young woman in love. She refused to worry about tomorrow.

Only yesterday she'd been in the middle of yet another attempted kidnapping. After her second debriefing in twenty-four hours, she was exhausted. The rest of her time had been spent with her mother, sleeping, shopping for her upcoming move, and trying to explain to Marcus why she couldn't tell him where the State Department was sending her. Oddly enough, he understood that part.

"I've spent nearly every single one of my years in service unable to tell my family and friends where I am, where I'm heading. It's part of my job. If the SD made you sign an NDA, you have to abide by it. The good news is they're granting both your asylum requests. I couldn't be happier about that. Plus, I know we'll find a way to see each other. You did say they told you calls out and letters were allowed, right?"

Fatima nodded. "But it's not the same as both of us knowing where the other is, being able to picture it, to easily reach out. You'll be sent out on another mission again, I suppose."

He'd taken her hand then. "Sure, but that's the life of a soldier. You know that. And I won't be able to tell you where I'm going."

"I know, but—"

Skyscraper saw the anguish in her eyes. He cupped her face gently, his thumb caressing her cheek. "We'll make it work. All it takes is for us both to want it. Do you want us to work, Fatima? Do you want me?"

Her heart leapt into her throat, and she swallowed. "Yes, Marcus, I do. I do want you. I want us."

He smiled, slow and sexy. "I sure do like hearing you say that. Say it again," he whispered.

Fatima bit her lip, suddenly shy, and yet, emboldened by the hunger in his amber eyes. "I want you, Marcus."

He kissed her then, long, slow, and deep. Each sweep of his tongue against hers sent lightning streaking throughout her body. Every caress of his lips against her skin, across her cheek, and down her neck made her yearn for more. Just as he pulled her close, pressed her body to his own, her mother interrupted from the next room.

"Time to say goodnight, Fatima. Tell your Marcus he will see you tomorrow."

It was like a bucket of cold water.

Skyscraper had laughed low in her ear. "I love your mama, but her timing sucks. Or maybe it's perfect. The jury is out on that one."

She'd floated on air the rest of the night and all the next day on that memory alone, and now they were on their first official date. No mother in sight.

The song came to an end. Marcus stood and took his bows, exiting the stage as the band struck up another bluesy jazz tune. Fatima couldn't help but notice he looked like a jungle cat approaching its prey. Her mouth went dry.

Skyscraper stopped in front of her extending his hand. "May I have this dance, Miss Ali?"

She placed her hand in his, rising. "You may, Mr. Du-Bose."

He led her onto the small dancefloor pulling her into his arms. "I've wanted to hold you all night."

"Well," she said, practicing flirtation, "you had to wine and dine me first. I'm not cheap, after all."

He grinned. "No, ma'am, you are worth that and so much more." His eyes raked her from head to toe. "You look like a princess. My God, how did I get so lucky?"

Fatima blushed. "You call it luck, and yet we both went through hell to get here, Marcus."

He kissed her fingers and placed her hand over his heart. "And I'd do it all again. I'd do it twice if it meant you never had to experience any of it."

The sincerity in his eyes touched her soul. He meant every word.

The music flowed, enticing them to follow the rhythm. There were other couples on the dance floor, but Fatima didn't notice. For her, there was only Marcus. In his arms, she felt safe, protected, and more turned on than she cared to admit. With every step, their bodies slid sensuously coming together like magnets. Parts of her melted while others throbbed painfully. This was new territory for her. Her sexual experiences thus far had been a few stolen kisses so easy to walk away from. Not so with Marcus. Her untried body yearned for more and she didn't know how to proceed.

But he did.

"Let's get out of here."

"Yes, let's," she agreed.

Skyscraper took her hand and led her off the dance floor and, after quickly dispensing with the check, out of the club. Outside, a chilly mist settled over D.C. Fatima pulled her wrap around her shoulders as Skyscraper hailed a taxi.

"Where are we going?" she asked.

He looked at her, hopeful. "My place?"

"You have a place here?" Her wide eyes expressed her surprise.

"Well, assigned temporary quarters as of yesterday, but they're mine until I bug out. We don't have to go there. I mean, I can take you back to the Ritz..."

"No," she said, taking his hand. "Let's go to your place."

He paused, surprised. "Okay." He turned giving the base address to the driver.

It was twenty of the longest minutes of Fatima's life before they arrived on base. The billeting quarters were simple, and Marcus's rooms were smaller than the hotel room she and her mother currently shared. Still, there was a living room, a kitchenette, and bedroom with a full bathroom. It was neat and clean, and she could smell a hint of his cologne on the air.

Nerves swamped her as he closed and locked the door.

"Can I get you something to drink? I think I have some bottled water and tea."

"I'm fine, really." She set her clutch bag down on the side table next to a stuffed chair.

He shoved his hands in his pockets, watching her. "We don't have to do anything, Fatima. I'm just happy being here with you. We can talk, not talk. Whatever. I mean, I get to spend time with the most beautiful lady in the world. This," he gestured between them, "is perfect. You're perfect."

His honesty touched her deeply, leaving her stunned. She couldn't find the words to express what was in her heart, so she took his hand and led him over to the sofa. She steered him around and placing both hands on his chest, pushed him down.

Skyscraper fell onto the seat cushion. Fatima stood before him removing the wrap from her shoulders, letting it slide to the floor. Slowly, she grabbed handfuls of her gown pulling the hem up to her knees. Then, she climbed onto his lap, straddling his hips.

He swallowed hard. "Fatima—"

"Sssh!" she placed a finger over his lips. Staring into his eyes, she said, "Marcus, make love to me."

The air whooshed from his lungs. Her bold actions were rivaled by a shyness in her lovely almond-shaped brown eyes. He knew she'd never before uttered those words. That she did so now struck him profoundly. She was a gift, a priceless treasure, and he knew he must handle her with the greatest care.

Skyscraper reached up and slid the straps of her gown down her shoulders. There was a zipper in the back, and when the material would not budge further, he slid his hands around her slim ribcage and unzipped the dress. Carefully, he peeled the gown down revealing her breasts.

Scars greeted his eyes. Cigarette burns. He remembered her telling him Omar had burned her in addition to the beatings and other abuse. Anger bubbled up but he forced it back down. The last thing she needed was to feel as if she weren't good enough, as if she wasn't beautiful. In his eyes, she was perfect. Her breasts were perfect. The scars only made her more amazing. They were a testament to her strength, her resilience, and her courage. He stared at her breasts in awe. Ripe, firm, and tan with dusky rose-colored nipples so hard, his mouth watered.

"You're beautiful," he muttered.

"Touch me, please," she whispered, longing in her tone.

Holding her gaze, he cupped her breasts, kneading them. Passion glazed her eyes and her lips parted. It was all the invitation he needed. He kissed her then, his hands still kneading her soft flesh, his fingers finding the stiff peaks, caressing and tweaking them. When she moaned into his mouth, his own passion rose another five notches. Twisting them both around, he laid her down on the couch. His hands captured hers stretching her arms above her head.

Skyscraper leaned down then and trailed kisses to her ear, down her neck, and over her chest.

Fatima could feel his hot breath hovering over her nipple. It was so erect, it hurt. She arched her back, silently begging him to relieve the sweet pain. His tongue shot out, licking the peak before his mouth closed over the mound sucking hard.

"Oh, yes!" she moaned.

She tasted so sweet, but he wanted more.

His lips worked their way down to her belly, tugging the dress further until he slid it beneath her bottom and off her legs. She lay before him wearing only a pair of lacy white panties. The scent of her sex filled his nostrils and intoxicated him.

Glancing up, he noted the look in her eyes, a combination of uncertainty and desire. Her cheeks were flushed, and her lips parted. Smiling, his head dipped low again. His lips skimmed a line from her bellybutton to the white lacy material. There, his fingers slid beneath and tugged until she was completely exposed.

Skyscraper caressed her legs before leaning back down and licking a hot line up the inside of her thigh. She trembled as the tip of his nose tickled the silken hairs of her mons. Her honey beckoned and his mouth watered. Slowly, he parted her womanly flesh and flicked his tongue over her sensitive nub.

A sharp pant greeted his ears, making him smile. He buried his face deep, this time tasting her sweetness in full. The sounds of her pleasure drove him crazy. Skyscraper gripped her hips, licking and sucking hard, taking her higher. He wanted her first experience to be nothing but ecstasy.

"Marcus," she panted, her hips thrusting as she squirmed, reaching for his shoulders. "Please!"

He knew what she wanted, what she needed. One hand reached for her breast, cupping the softness of her warm skin. His fingers found her nipple and pinched as he continued lapping her honey.

"Yes, oh, yes! Oh, my God," she moaned. Fatima's body tightened, and then exploded as her first orgasm wracked her nubile body.

Skyscraper licked her nub eliciting powerful sensations that had her calling his name.

She was breathless and trembling, and as he pulled back to stare up at her, he knew she was the most beautiful woman he'd ever seen.

He sat back and waited for her to catch her breath.

Fatima looked at him, her face aglow. She saw the desire in his eyes, and the evidence of his arousal lower. Her eyes widened. Now would be the time to stop, but she didn't want to stop.

"What about you?" she asked.

"Don't worry about me," he smiled. "Tonight is about you."

She sat up. "No. Tonight is about us." She stood and took his hand leading him into the bedroom. She knew it was right. The right time. The right man.

That night, she gave herself fully, body and soul to the man she loved. Her Marcus.

The morning sun trickled through the blinds dotting the floor with bright spots. Fatima watched as dust danced in the dim rays. Behind her, Marcus slept, his arm around her waist, holding her close. Her body ached in unfamiliar places, but it was a sweet ache, one that reminded her she'd been completely and thoroughly loved. She smiled recalling how he'd touched her, caressed her body, how it felt when he'd entered her for the first time. The small amount of pain at the passing of her virginity was worth it for the pleasure he'd given with every stroke. She still couldn't believe it. The memory of the things he'd done to her with his tongue caused heat to rise in her cheeks. Knowing the physical side of love now, she didn't know how she would handle being apart from him.

Something hard pressed against her backside. Marcus was awake, or, at least, part of him was.

"Good morning, beautiful," he whispered near her ear.

Fatima turned her head and was greeted with a soft kiss. "Good morning, Marcus."

"It is a good morning," he said, voice low. "Let's make it better." He pulled her atop him and with a quick motion, slid deep within her.

"Oh, my God!" she arched her back, her hands on his chest for support.

He was immediately contrite. "I'm sorry. Are you sore?" He started to pull out, but she stopped him.

"What? No." She sat up, riding him. "No, no, no, not sore," she sang.

The pleasure generated by her hip thrusts robbed him of speech. All he could do was grip her waist and let her take the lead. He managed to mutter, "Oh, thank you, Jesus."

He watched her as she took her own pleasure. The sight of her sensuous movements threatened to push him over the edge, but he wanted her to climax first. Slyly, he slid a finger down between them, and finding her nub, rubbed the sensitive area in time to her rhythm. Within minutes, her body shuddered, spasming around him. It was too much to bear, and he spilled his seed.

She fell atop him as they both fought to catch their breath.

Skyscraper wound a strand of her hair around his fingers. "You know, we didn't use protection just now."

Fatima turned her face to look at him. "You're worried I might get pregnant?"

"I'm more worried your mama and my mama will take turns kicking my ass if you do."

She laughed, but then grew serious. "Marcus, this was my choice. If I do, I don't expect anything—"

"Hold on there," he said, lifting her chin. "It wasn't just your choice. I have a say too. And I'm not worried about you getting pregnant, Miss Ali. I mean, unless you don't want that, and that would be a different matter."

She sat up. "Marcus," she said, searching his eyes. "Are you saying you would want that?"

"I'm saying I'm not going anywhere, but..."

"But what?" Sitting up, she placed her hands on her hips, staring down at him.

Marcus grinned. She looked ready to choke him. "I just want us to do things the right way. You know, dating, marriage, and then, God willing, have children."

Fatima's eyes narrowed. "Didn't we just go on a first date last night? Looks like you've jumped the gun."

"Well, to be fair, you did ask me to make love to you," he teased.

"Marcus!" she slapped his chest.

"Ow!" he said, laughing. Then, he turned serious, taking her hands. "Fatima Ali, you're not making it easy to ask you to marry me."

The air left her lungs. Inhaling deeply, she said, "Are you asking?"

He held her gaze. "I am," he said, pulling her close and wrapping his arms around her. "Fatima, there's been something real, something solid and strong between us since I first laid eyes on you. You're so amazing, so brave, and you accept me for who I am, bad stuff and all. I love being with you, love talking to you. I love you. I want to spend the rest of my life getting to know everything about you. Will you marry me?"

Tears welled in her eyes, and she glowed with happiness. "I...a ring. There's supposed to be a ring, isn't there?"

Marcus looked around the room. On the nightstand sat his cuff links. They weren't a ring, but at the moment, they were all the jewelry he had. He reached for them. "Okay, so these obviously are not a ring, but they're old and belonged to my granddad and then my dad. Until I can buy you the most beautiful princess ring in the world, I want you to hold onto these. They mean the world to me, and so do you. Now will you marry me?"

She grinned, holding the cuff links close to her heart. Taking a deep breath, she gave him an answer.

"Yes. Yes, Marcus, I will marry you."

"You will? Oh, my God!" He hugged her tight, kissing her lips. "I love you so much!"

Fatima grew dizzy, joy filling her. "You still have to ask my mother, you know."

"Then let's go ask her." He got up, pulling Fatima along with him.

"We can't go like this, Marcus!" She laughed, pointing out their nakedness.

His eyes raked her from head to toe. "No, I guess not. So, we'll shower first, and then I can go prostrate myself before your mom."

Marcus led Fatima to the bathroom. As the steam from their shower spilled out into the room, the two lovers lathered, laughed, and loved.

A stray thought niggled its way into her mind. As they rinsed away the suds she said, "You know, now I'll get to tell you where they're sending me."

"I'll have to sign a nondisclosure first, but yeah. That's how it works."

"I can't wait."

He winked. "But you will. You're part of my crazy government world now, baby. And I'm part of yours. I admit, though, I'm curious."

She threw him a towel. "Well, then, hurry up. The sooner you get my mother's blessing, the sooner we begin our lives together."

"Yes, ma'am," he grinned. "I sure do like this side of you, Miss Ali." He spun her around, gently buffing her backside with the towel. "And I like this side too."

"Marcus!"

"I love when you say my name, baby. And I love you, Fatima Ali."

She snuggled close to his naked chest. "I love you, too, Marcus DuBose."

"We're going to be one badass couple," he said, looking down into her upturned face. "And our children," he grinned. "They are going to be amazing. Smart and beautiful like their mama."

She laughed. "Can we get married first before you have me barefoot and pregnant?"

"Yes, we can. I'm just excited, is all." He moved, gently taking her hand, and beginning to dance.

"Oh, Marcus, you're making me believe in fairytales. Look at us. Dancing naked in your bathroom and planning a family."

He stepped out and spun her around before reeling her back in. "Best day of my life, Fatima. Can't wait to call you Mrs. DuBose." He dipped her back. "Can't wait to call you mine."

Fatima's heart skipped a beat. "You can start now, my love."

Chapter 19

Outlaw exited the cab and hoisted his duffel bag over his shoulder. As the taxi drove away, he stood before the two-story red brick house on Aspen Lane. Excitement filled him. So did guilt.

Two weeks. Two long weeks passed since his son had been born. He should have been here, been by Emma's side, holding her hand.

What if something had happened to her, or to his son? The thought made him sick to his stomach. They'd needed him, and he'd been halfway around the world chasing down extremists to save someone else's child. How did he reconcile what he swore and oath to do and who he swore another oath to? Defend the constitution against enemies foreign and domestic, and love, honor, and cherish...until death do they part. The two oaths, both noble, had clashed, and only one could be fulfilled at the time. If he could carbon copy himself, he could do both. But that was wishful thinking, and this was reality.

Outlaw looked down at the Teddy bear in his hand. The small brown bear wore a black bowtie with white music symbols on it. He'd picked it up at the airport in D.C. before flying out to Denver. He hadn't really thought about why this particular bear caught his eye in the gift shop, but now that he had a moment to reflect, he smiled. He'd been in New Orleans when he found out he had a son. The music symbols reminded him of the city, and the city was the place where he'd received the amazing, joyous news.

He'd been excited to get back home and meet him, to see Emma again. But now that he stood just outside the red brick house, his guilt stopped him.

And it was more than the fact that he'd missed the birth. He knew it.

Outlaw stared at the bear. "Charlie," he whispered, pain cutting through his heart.

Memories of his first child, his daughter, Charlotte—called Charlie—came flooding back. Her death, caused by a gunshot wound fired by a thief inside the U.S. illegally, who'd attempted to rob his ex-wife while she walked home from Charlie's birthday party, haunted him still. He had never forgiven himself for not being there then, once again called away to duty. But for a while, he'd thought about her a little less. Happiness came back into his life with Emma, and then it grew exponentially when she told him she was pregnant. He'd been thrilled!

Then guilt trickled back in. How dare he be happy when Charlie was dead? The struggle within raged on, and now it paralyzed him. He couldn't put one foot in front of the other right now even if an army of insurgents were at his back.

The front door cracked open and a familiar face peeked out. Glasses slid down her nose and she quickly pushed them back up.

"Nate?" she asked, her dark eyes wide. "You're home?"

A smile spread across Emma's face as she bounded down the porch and ran down the sidewalk.

Her body hit his with enthusiastic force, her arms winding around his neck and her legs jumping up and locking around his waist.

He held on for dear life.

"When?" she asked, squeezing his neck.

"Just now," he mumbled, inhaling the fragrance of her hair. Her scent, her warmth, melted into him and his paralysis faded.

Emma leaned back and looked at her man, smiling. "I've missed you so much!"

Outlaw's heart slammed into his chest. *What had he ever done to deserve this woman?*

"I've miss you like hell," he whispered, and then kissed her. Passion blazed between them as two lovers reconnected and rediscovered each other. Every ounce of love he felt for Emma was poured into that kiss, leaving them both breathless.

Finally, he pulled away and stared down into her eyes.

"I'm sorry I wasn't here," he said.

Emma touched his cheek. "It's okay. I understand."

Nate touched his forehead to hers. "It's not okay. I should've been here."

Her voice low and soothing, she replied, "You couldn't help it, Nate. And I'm okay. We're okay," she said, her arms grasping his shoulders and holding him close.

Outlaw sucked in a deep breath. His eyes stung and he closed them tight, not ready to let go of his love just yet.

Emma felt something tickle her ear and turned her head. She came face to face with a Teddy bear and smiled.

"Is that for the baby?"

He loosened his hold. A sheepish smile tugged at his lips. "It's not much. I didn't have time yet..."

Emma looked at him. "Do you want to meet your son, Nate?" she asked, her smile growing.

"I do. So much."

She pulled away, taking his hand. "Come on."

Outlaw let her pull him along, his feet now moving freely.

Inside, the familiarity of home greeted him. The furniture they'd picked out together, their pictures on the walls, and the scents of vanilla candles mixing with the cuts of pine tree boughs soothed his soul.

He dropped his duffel bag by the door, kicking it closed once they were in the house. Emma led the way upstairs. He watched her backside with deep appreciation, his mind suddenly recalling other things he'd missed while away.

She stopped at the top of the stairs and turned left. This was two of three bedrooms, and the one in which they'd painted a light green with white trim before he'd gone off on his last mission. Then, there'd been no furniture, but now, a white crib sat against the far wall, a mobile with cute zoo animals hanging over it.

Emma walked to the crib and leaned down over the rail.

"There's my little man," she cooed. "All awake after your nap?" She lifted the baby out and turned to Nate.

Outlaw stared down at the tiny bundle in Emma's arms. He wore a blue onesie. Arms and legs squirmed as the baby made small noises. Light brown hair sparsely covered his perfect head, and chubby cheeks rounded out his perfect face.

Emma approached and gestured for Nate to take him.

"This is your son, honey. Nathan James Oliver Junior."

Outlaw cradled the tiny boy in his hands, supporting the neck. He seemed so small, and yet, he was solid, and strong. An itty bitty hand wrapped around his finger and blue eyes stared up at him, wide with curiosity.

"My son," he whispered. Joy filled his heart once again. It was both a familiar feeling and entirely new. He'd had a daughter, and now a son. He couldn't be there to protect the first, but he promised himself in this moment, he would do everything in his power to protect his second child.

Emma watched as her big, muscled man held his newborn son. There were tears in his eyes, and she felt the sting of her own at the sight. She wrapped her arms around Nate's waist, grinning.

"My boys," she murmured.

Outlaw kissed the top of her head, then leaned down and kissed the baby's. "I love you both so much. My God, Emma, he's perfect. Just perfect. Look how strong he is already," he added, wiggling the finger that Nate Jr. had yet to relinquish. "I think he likes me," he said, his voice catching.

Emma chuckled. "Of course he does. You're his daddy."

A grin split Outlaw's face. "I'm your daddy," he said, talking to the baby. "Yes, I am." He maneuvered the baby into the crook of his arm, freeing the hand holding the Teddy bear by one leg. "And this is for you, son. His name is Jazzybear." He waved the bear back and forth drawing the baby's eyes away from him.

Nate Jr. eyed the bear, and a small smile tugged his baby lips over toothless gums.

"He's smiling! Emma, he's smiling!"

She laughed. "Yes. Probably gas, though."

"Can't be as bad as Hollywood's," he said, a chuckle escaping him.

Outlaw turned his attention to the room, looking beyond the crib to the rocking chair with a small side table. A changing table occupied one corner, and pictures hung on the wall above it. He stepped closer to look.

One was of him and Emma in D.C. the night of their first official date. Another was of the two of them when they moved into this house. The last, though, got him right in the heart. In black and white, and prominently placed in the middle, was a picture of Charlie. Golden curls and big eyes stared back at him, and a lump formed in his throat.

Emma's fingers slipped around his arm as she leaned her head against his shoulder.

"I hope you don't mind. I found this one when I was putting away all our things. I wanted Nate Jr. to know his sister. Now, she can always watch over him."

The stinging in Outlaw's eyes turned to a flood. The tears slipped down his cheeks, but the pain he expected from seeing her sweet face did not come. Instead, a feeling of peace took over and the weight of loss, of guilt lifted from his heart.

He slipped an arm around Emma and hugged her close. "I don't mind at all, Emma. It's perfect." He sniffed and looked at his son. "That's your big sister Charlie. She's your guardian angel now," he whispered.

They stood that way, together, filled with love, grateful for all they had.

Finally, Outlaw broke the silence.

"Marcus met a girl."

Surprised, Emma looked up. "What? Tell me all about it."

Emma took Nate's hand, leading him and the baby out of the room and back down the stairs. As she prepared the baby's bottle, Outlaw told her what he could about Skyscraper and Fatima Ali. Before long, he had his cellphone out and they got the entire team on a conference Zoom call where everyone met the newest addition to the team.

Fatima was with Marcus, and she and Emma hit it off right away.

Nate sat at the breakfast bar watching Emma and Fatima chat while she fed Nate Jr. In the background, Skyscraper looked over his lady's shoulder at Nate. The two men shared a moment, both recognizing how lucky they were. Skyscraper nodded at Outlaw, who grinned, and then both looked at Doc. The threesome turned their eyes to Ghost, Hollywood, Badger, and Jersey.

Outlaw pointed at each single man. "You're next."

The End

Afterword

Dear reader,

Sgt. Harold Tyler's, aka Eastwood's, story continues in my spinoff series, The Soldiers of PATCH-COM. Visit my website and get Secondhand Soldier, Book 1, in this exciting new series dedicated to our wounded warriors.

www.micheleegwynnauthor.com

Thanks for adding me to your 'To Be Read' list! And don't forget to click the "GET A FREE BOOK" tab at the top of my webpage to get your FREE book (choice of two different full stories).

~ Michele

Sneak Peek

Enjoy this sneak peek of book 4 in the Green Beret series, Saving Christmas.

Stiffed again. Christmas Jones removed the empty coffee mug and pie plate from the table, grumbling under her breath. She hated the holidays. New York City attracted more tourists in the weeks leading up to Christmas. For retailers, it was a blessing. For Frankie's Diner, it was a curse. For Chris, it meant getting stiffed on tips by chintzy tourists who figured they could get away with being jerks. Her regulars still came by, but usually less often to avoid the crowds or to spend time with loved ones. This meant she had to hustle twice as hard to earn her usual income in order to pay exorbitant rent on a shoebox apartment. It also meant she was not in the mood for Frankie's annual holiday joke.

"Hey, kid," he said, turning up the antique radio on the counter. "It's beginning to look a lot like Christmas." He sang the tune, a big smile on his wrinkled face. His serenading failed to pull her from her foul mood. Frankie DeSanti sighed. At sixty-nine, he'd owned and run Frankie's Diner in Brooklyn for thirty years. Before him, it was Ernie's Place, owned by Frankie's uncle Ernie Russo. Ernie never had any children. When he died, he left the diner to Frankie who renamed it, but kept the same menu to honor his uncle. Italian and American comfort foods were served along with the best coffee in the neighborhood and, local legendary baker, Miss Evangeline's homemade pies.

Chris deposited the dirty dishes in the kitchen. Big Mike picked them up and placed them in the sink, washing away the food debris. He'd been with Frankie for twenty of his thirty years of business, quietly washing the dishes every day. Chris couldn't even remember a day in the three years she'd worked here when Big Mike wasn't in the kitchen scrubbing food off plates and forks and knives. He always wore yellow rubber gloves and a green bandana tied around his balding head. A few wisps of gray hair poked out around his large ears, but she'd never seen him without his head covered. He didn't speak much either, but he wasn't mute. If Big Mike had something to say, a person ought to listen. He observed everything, never missing a detail; a fact realized when he did open his mouth. Because his words were so few, they carried a lot of weight, and he only shared them when he felt it was important.

Now was not one of those times. Chris returned to the front. In addition to the booths, the diner had an old-fashioned counter with a row of barstools riveted to the floor. A man sat at the end of the row sipping coffee. He'd been in every day over the past two weeks. He sat in the same spot and ordered the same thing; a cup of coffee and a slice of hot apple pie. He had a rough look about him, like a life hard lived. Dingy gray strands mingled with his dark hair. He needed a haircut, but it was the scar on his right cheek that stood out. The jagged cut zig-zagged over his cheekbone off into his hairline. The skin around it was puckered like it hadn't healed properly. It looked painful. Besides the scar, old tattoos littered his hands continuing up under the sleeves of his black leather jacket. Prison tats, she guessed. The only jewelry he wore was a gold crucifix around his neck.

She normally wouldn't have noticed so much about a customer, especially a new one, but this man creeped her out. It wasn't his tattoos or even his scary scar. It was the way he looked at her. She'd felt his eyes on her every time he came in, but when she turned to look his way, he was always staring down at his plate or his coffee cup. She mentioned it to Big Mike after the third day. He looked out through the pass-through from the kitchen, observing the man a moment, and then shrugged. Chris figured if Big Mike didn't notice anything off about the strange man, then she shouldn't worry about him either. It was good advice, so why did she still feel creeped out?

Customers coming through the door pulled Chris's attention away from the creepy man. A gust of cold wind followed a small group of people inside. They waited to be seated before noticing the sign that read "Seat Yourself."

Tourists, she thought, shaking her head. Another man came in behind them. He noticed the sign right away. Chris noticed him.

He looked like Captain America. Tall, dark blond, and broad-shouldered. He had the face of a model, but the haircut and bearing of a military man. He looked around the crowded interior before deciding on a stool at the counter. There were only three left. He chose the empty one two seats over from the creep. Shrugging out of his leather jacket, he placed it over the back of the stool, and dropped a military duffel bag on the open seat to the right.

Chris noticed the size of his arms beneath the thermal weave of his black Henley. He obviously worked out. She sighed, appreciating the eye candy he provided. Not that a guy like that would ever notice her, but maybe her day was about to improve. She pulled the pad out of her apron pocket and walked his way.

"Welcome to Frankie's. What can I get for you?"

The handsome man scanned the menu on the wall, then answered, "Coffee, black, and a slice of Miss Evangeline's lemon meringue pie please."

Surprised, Chris asked, "You know Miss Evangeline?" Most people didn't notice where the pies came from, only the variety.

He looked up, his eyes taking her in. Chris noticed they were as blue as the ocean, fringed in dark lashes.

The man gave her a quick once-over lingering a half-second longer than necessary on her breasts before locking eyes. He smiled and Chris felt her cheeks warm.

"Of course. I grew up on Miss E's pies. She's the best."

"You're from here? I've never seen you before," she said.

"Been overseas the past few years. This is the first trip home I've had in a while." He extended his hand. "Shane McCall."

She hesitated, then placed her hand in his. It was warm but rough, his grip firm. "Chris Jones. Military?"

"Yes ma'am," he said. Her stomach did a happy flip. "U.S. Army Green Beret."

"Sounds intense. What do you do in the army?"

He grinned. "Whatever my commanders tell me, ma'am." Shane gave the usual reply.

Chris knew he was messing with her. She shook her head, a half-smile on her lips. "Well, Shane, welcome home. I'll get your order right out to you."

"Thank you, ma'am," he said, watching her leave, an appreciative smile on his handsome face.

Chris felt his eyes on her and blushed. It was a good thing he couldn't see her face. She reached up to grab a coffee mug and filled it to the rim. Then, she plated a thick slice of lemon meringue pie, just a bit larger than a normal slice, and carried them both back to the good-looking soldier. It wasn't everyday she encountered such a gorgeous man. Heck, it wasn't even every month. She hadn't dated at all in over a year, blaming her work schedule. She worked as many hours as Frankie would allow overtime trying to make ends meet. That left no time in between for a personal life. At least, that's what she told herself. It was easier than facing the fact that men didn't usually pay her any attention. They liked her well enough, but apparently not enough to ask her out. She tried not to dwell on it, but now and again, old wounds reopened reminding her she wasn't any man's first choice. Still, feeling Captain America's blue eyes upon her reminded her of what she'd been missing.

She told herself he was just playing around and not being serious at all.

"One coffee, black, and one big slice of Miss Evangeline's lemon meringue pie as ordered." She set the items down in front of him. "There's sugar and cream here if you need them," she added, pointing to the carousel on the counter.

"Christmas Jones?"

A man wearing a long Navy-blue coat over a dark suit approached. He was mid-fifties, dark-haired, and resembled a character from a Godfather movie.

"Yes?" she replied, surprised. She had no idea who this man was or how he knew her full name. Other than Frankie and Big Mike, no one else in the diner knew her first name was Christmas.

He pulled an envelope from the inside breast pocket of his jacket. It was a thick, cream-colored vellum and looked official. "This is for you." He pulled out a card adding it to the envelope which he handed over. "If you have any questions, call the number on the card." He turned to leave.

"Wait! What's this about? Am I in trouble?" She had no idea what was going on.

He glanced over his shoulder. "All I know is that envelope is for Christmas Jones. You're Christmas Jones. Any questions, call the number on the card. Good day, miss." He left her standing there holding the official-looking cream-colored envelope.

Chris stared at it like it was a snake that might bite. Her name was typed on the outside along with the hand-written words, "To be opened on your twenty-fifth birthday." Her birthday was tomorrow. December the 8ᵗʰ. She had no idea who it was from or what it was about. She glanced at the card. The name Leo Profacci was embossed in gold lettering. Beneath the name it read *Attorney at Law*. But it didn't say for whom or for which firm. There was a phone number and nothing else.

"Everything okay?"

Chris looked at the soldier. She shrugged. "I don't know. I don't know what that was about," she said, putting the envelope into the pocket of the apron tied around her waist. Reaching up, she tightened her ponytail and then tugged the hem of her blue sweater down over her jeans.

He pointed at her pocket with his fork. "Then I suspect you'll find the answers inside that envelope."

"Yeah, I guess so." Absently, Chris reached for her necklace. It was a silver medallion with a blue enamel rendering of the Virgin Mary. She rubbed it with her thumb, her thoughts all over the map.

He watched her. "So, Christmas, is it?"

"What?" she refocused her attention outward. "Oh, yeah."

"Your parents big fans of the holiday or something?"

She stiffened, dropping the necklace back down into her shirt. "I don't know. The nuns named me. I was found on their doorstep on Christmas morning."

Shane McCall put down his fork. Quietly, he said, "I'm sorry. I shouldn't have pried."

"It's okay—"

The creepy man with the hideous scar lunged across the counter reaching for her neck...

Download Saving Christmas by visiting my website now!

www.micheleegwynnauthor.com

Also By Michele E. Gwynn

Did you miss books I-V in the Green Beret Series? Grab them now! Rescuing Emma, Loving Leisl, Freeing Fatima, Saving Christmas, and Loving Freddie, newly remastered and re-edited with bonus scenes. The Green Beret series was previously written as part of the special forces world created by NYT Bestselling Author Susan Stoker. The series is now re-edited outside of Stoker's world with an all-new SEAL teams as a point of contact/support team to Outlaw's Green Berets: Visit micheleegwynnauthor.com.

The Soldiers of PATCH-COM is the spinoff series from Gwynn's Green Beret series. Secondhand Soldier is the debut book. Keep up with new releases in this series by signing up for my newsletter.

Checkpoint Novels

Exposed: The Education of Sarah Brown (novel)
The Evolution of Elsa Kreiss (novel)
The Redemption of Joseph Heinz (novel)
The Making of Herman Faust (prequel novella)

Green Beret Series

Rescuing Emma (18+)
Loving Leisl
Freeing Fatima
Saving Christmas
Loving Freddie
*Saving Major Morgan (A Green Beret Series prequel novel-
la)*

The Soldiers of PATCH-COM

Secondhand Soldier (18+)
Second Chance Soldier
Second Breath Soldier
Silent Night Soldier
C'est la Vie Soldier (Coming Soon)

The Harvest Trilogy

Harvest (audiobook available free on my YouTube channel)
Hybrids
Census

Section 5 (A Harvest Trilogy Spinoff)

Angelic Hosts Series

Camael's Gift (audiobook available on my YouTube channel)
Camael's Battle (audiobook available on my YouTube channel)
Sophie's Wish
Nephilim Rising

Stand Alones

Darkest Communion (Paranormal Romance, 18+)
Waiting a Lifetime (Contemporary Romance, Mystical)
Hiring John (Romantic Comedy 18+)